# For Better or Worse

# For Better or Worse

A John Bekker Mystery

## Al Lamanda

Encircle Publications, LLC
Farmington, Maine U.S.A.

# Chapter One

The eight-ounce ankle weights I wore felt like eight pounds after thirty minutes of jogging along the shoreline at the beach.

The late afternoon sun was low and warm in the sky. I checked my watch and at the thirty-minute mark, I turned around and headed back. With around a hundred yards to go, I slowed my pace to a walk and allowed my daughter Regan's dog to run to me and escort me home.

He's a little pug with the energy of a freight train and if his little legs could keep up, he'd run the entire way with me.

We reached home, or what used to be, a thirty-year-old, somewhat seedy trailer set back about a hundred yards from the ocean.

I purchased it about fifteen years ago after my wife was murdered by the very criminals I was investigating. They broke into my home, murdered my wife and by some miracle, overlooked my five-year-old daughter, who was hiding in a closet.

The end result of that was a decade long drinking binge during which time I lost everything. My house, my job as a police detective, and my daughter. While I was off drinking, she was existing in a special hospital for traumatized children.

The bank took the house, the city took my job, the hospital took my daughter, and I would have been homeless on the street if my wife's sister, Janet, hadn't stepped in and taken control of the situation.

Maybe thirty years ago, this section of beach was deemed worthless because of rocks and waves too strong for any but the die-hard surfer. Some developer pitched an idea to the town council. He wanted to sell mobile-style homes to surfers as timeshares. Twenty were placed along this stretch of beach and sold for a hundred thousand each. The town council got greased by the developer, and the town collected a hundred thousand in property taxes every year.

By the time I was sucking down a quart of scotch every day, the surfing crowd had moved on to greener pastures and more exciting waves, and Janet was able to buy a trailer for me using my pension fund.

And thank God that she did.

A few years after I moved in, there were just two trailers left on the beach. Mine and one a hundred yards or so to the right belonging to an elderly black man named Oz.

Oz had his own problems to cope with, and we coped together just about every night by drinking until we passed out cold.

Salvation came from the oddest of places. The very mobster I was investigating and who I believed was responsible for my wife's murder had me kidnapped and cleaned up and then hired me to find my wife's murderer.

His name was Eddie Crist and he was dying of cancer and didn't want to check out without knowing who was behind it all.

The short of it was that I exposed the corrupt cops in the department that cleared Crist just weeks before he died, and I got my life back, somewhat.

Working as a private investigator to supplement my police pension, I was able to buy a home a few miles up the beach that has a view but no access to the water. Regan is nineteen now and lives with me.

So does Oz, as he is family.

I kept the trailer and use it as an office.

But that, too, is about to change.

Another developer sold an idea to the town council. Beachfront condos. I was given sixty days to remove the trailer or they would do it for me. The notice came a week ago by registered mail.

When I reached the trailer, Oz and Regan were sitting in beach chairs. Molly, our cat, jumped down from Regan's lap to play tag with the pug, who Regan named Cuddles.

"Dad, can they really take the trailer away from us?" Regan said.

"They can and they will," I said. "But they'll have to buy us out first."

"But, dad, how can they...?" Regan said.

"Everything changes, honey," I said. "Some changes we like, some we don't, but nothing ever stands still."

Fed up with the pug, Molly jumped onto Oz's lap.

"We change, everything change along with us," Oz said as Molly rubbed her ears against his stomach.

Oz tended to speak in short, truncated sentences, but he was smart as a whip and had a dry sense of humor.

"Well, when are we going for breakfast?" Regan said.

"As soon as Jane and your Uncle Walt get here," I said.

On the side of the trailer is an old suspended heavy bag and a pair of elevated push-up bars. I went around, slipped on my twenty-year-old bag gloves and went to work on the bag.

I got in fifteen minutes on the bag and several sets of push-ups before Walt arrived.

I heard him say, "Where's the ugly one?"

"Follow the grunts and groans to the pot of gold," Oz said.

I was just standing up when Walt walked over to me.

"Don't you ever get sick of sweating?" he said.

"A little exercise wouldn't hurt that gut of yours," I said.

Walt grabbed the roll around his middle. "This is *fun* fat," he said. "The reason you don't have any is you never have any fun."

"Grab a cup of coffee while I take a quick shower," I said.

When I emerged from the trailer, showered and changed, Sheriff Jane Morgan had arrived and was seated next to Oz.

"Sorry about the trailer," Jane said. "I made a few calls. The town council won't budge when they smell found money."

Jane Morgan has been the county sheriff for over a decade. She's north of forty-five, blonde, and has been described as Marylyn Monroe in a sheriff's uniform. We've known each other for twenty years, but only recently became an item. It was her day off and she wore jeans and a sweatshirt, which did little to hide her ample figure.

"It's okay," I said. "Let's get some breakfast."

"Who pays?" Walt said.

We converged on a large diner a few blocks from the beach. We left the pets in the trailer with the promise of bacon as a reward.

Oz ordered an omelet with bacon, hash browns, and buttered toast, and Regan had a fit just short of a meltdown.

Three months ago, Oz suffered a minor heart attack. Doctors cleared a blockage from an artery and he was home within forty-eight hours. His most recent checkup was a week ago and he was given a clean bill of health, which is amazing when you consider how much we drank over a decade.

Regan forced Oz to settle for a virgin omelet and turkey bacon.

"Girl, even the cat won't eat no turkey bacon," Oz said.

The conversation turned to Walt's retirement.

"Twenty-nine days and a wakeup," Walt said.

"And then?" Jane asked.

"Elizabeth has a two-week cruise planned to the Caribbean," Walt said.

"And then?" Jane said.

"I don't know," Walt said. "I'm too young to sit around watching game shows all day. Maybe a corporate security job if I can find one."

"Why can't you partner up with Jack?" Jane said.

"Get real, Jane," Walt said. "After thirty years on the job, do you think I want to start all over again with Dick Tracy here?"

"Actually, Walt, that's not a bad idea," I said. "You work for who you want to work for, when you want and the pay is pretty good."

Walt looked at me. "I'll give it some thought," he said.

After breakfast, Walt drove to the police station, while the rest of us returned to the beach.

Oz was correct, the cat turned her nose up at the turkey bacon, but the pug wolfed it down.

Jane, Regan and I changed into bathing suits, rode the waves for a bit, and relaxed in the sun.

Oz took a nap in his chair with Molly on his lap.

It was one of those perfect summer days that you wished could last forever.

It is amazing how things can change on a dime.

# Chapter Two

When I bought the house, I made sure I looked for one with three bedrooms, a finished basement, a decent sized backyard with a fence, and a view of the ocean from the second floor.

The basement became my working office and the backyard my gym. I had a heavy bag/speed bag combo on a tripod, elevated push-up bars, a pull-up rack, a bench with a row of dumbbells, and several types of jump ropes.

I was working the heavy bag after breakfast when Regan came outside with my cell phone.

"Jane," Regan said. "She sounds upset."

I took the phone. "Jane?"

"Quit punching shit and get down here right away," Jane said.

"'Here' being?"

"County lockup, asshole, where else?" Jane said. "And hurry."

"Why?"

"Walt has been arrested and is waiting arraignment," Jane said.

* * *

By the time I reached the county jail where Walt was being held, he had been transported to the courthouse for arraignment.

Jane was out front, standing beside her cruiser.

I parked, got out and got in, and before I could buckle the seat belt, she had slammed down on the gas.

She hit the lights, lit a cigarette and said, "They raided his house at six this morning."

"Who?"

"I.A.D.," Jane said. "And a dozen members of SWAT from another precinct."

"A dozen? What did they charge him with?" I said.

"I don't know," Jane said. "I guess we'll find out at the arraignment."

"They arrested him at his home, transported him to the county jail, and didn't tell you why?" I said.

"I wasn't even there yet," Jane said. "And they didn't tell my deputies."

"Traffic, Jane. Hit the wailer," I said.

Jane hit the wailer and traffic parted.

"Fucking *move*," Jane snarled as she exhaled smoke through her nose.

"Walt is the most honest man I know," I said. "What could I.A.D. have on him that they raided his house at dawn?"

Jane glanced at me. "He was in his fucking pajamas for God's sake."

"Step on it, let's go," I said.

"You want me to drive on the sidewalk?" Jane said.

"You can ride on a magic carpet, just get us there," I said.

Jane got us there. She parked in the area reserved for police vehicles, and then we raced up the courthouse steps and entered the courthouse.

Elizabeth, Walt's wife of thirty-two years, was sitting on a bench outside the arraignment courtroom, holding a brown shopping bag on her lap.

She jumped to her feet when she spotted us walking toward her.

"Jack, Sheriff Morgan, I don't know what to say," Elizabeth said.

"When is he being arraigned?" I said.

"Not for an hour," Elizabeth said.

I took Elizabeth's arm and guided us to the cafeteria down the hall. I got three coffees and we found a table.

"Tell us everything," I said.

Elizabeth's hands shook a bit as she took a sip of coffee. "At six this morning, they smashed in the front door with one of those battering rams," she said. "They said it's because Walt has guns in the house. They had a warrant."

"What did it say, the warrant?" I said.

"I don't know. Something about the right to search the house," Elizabeth said. "I only glanced at it."

"When they arrested Walt, what were the charges?" I said.

"Something about extortion, criminal activity, bribery," Elizabeth said as she held back tears. "It happened so fast, I don't remember much. I'm sorry."

"Did they take anything from the house?" I said.

"From the garage," Elizabeth said. "A box they said had fifty thousand dollars in it."

"A box? What kind of box?" I said.

"Like a strong box," Elizabeth said.

"Have you ever seen it before?" I said.

"No."

"What's in the shopping bag?"

"Clothes," Elizabeth said. "They took him out in his pajamas."

"Do you know who his lawyer is?" I said.

Elizabeth shook her head. Her eyes were bloodshot, her face creased with worry lines. "I don't know a damn thing, Jack. Not a goddamn thing."

I looked at Jane. "See what you can find out," I said.

Jane stood up. "I'll meet you in the courtroom," she said.

After Jane left, I said, "Elizabeth, did you see the fifty thousand in the strong box?"

She nodded. Then the tears began to flow.

"Liz," I said. "I know this is hard, but you have to pull yourself together and be strong. All the tears in the world won't help Walt right now."

Elizabeth nodded. "Give me a minute," she said.

* * *

Jane was on a bench outside the courtroom with Walt's union appointed lawyer. He was young, still in his thirties. He stood up when Elizabeth and I arrived.

"I'm Harry Kane, Mr. Grimes's lawyer," he said.

"How old are you?" I said.

"Thirty-six. Why?" Harry said.

"It speaks to experience," I said.

"I've been with the department five years," Harry said. "I assure you I wouldn't have been assigned to this case had I not been qualified."

"What are the charges?" I said.

"Bribery, extortion, racketeering, conspiring with known mobsters, and money laundering," Harry said.

"What is the evidence?" I said.

"Fifty thousand found in the garage and six hundred thousand in a safe deposit box in the Cayman Islands," Harry said.

"We've never been to the Cayman Islands," Elizabeth said. "Walt's passport expired ten years ago. I've been after him to renew it so we could take a cruise after his retirement."

"The FBI traveled to the Cayman Islands and found the safety deposit box with six hundred thousand dollars in it under Captain Grimes's name," Harry said. "The bank identified him by photograph, and the signature on the account paperwork is a match."

"That's impossible," Elizabeth said. "I would know if Walt went to the Cayman Islands, for God's sake."

"I have to go in," Harry said. "He's up next."

Jane and Elizabeth followed me inside the courtroom and we sat directly behind Walt and Harry.

I looked at the ADA as he and Harry and Walt approached the bench. He wasn't the normal second-stringer usually sent for an arraignment hearing, but rather, the senior Assistant District Attorney.

"How does the defendant plead?" the judge said.

"Not guilty," Walt said.

"Your honor, the People request five hundred thousand dollars bail," the ADA said.

"That's ridiculous," Harry said. "Your honor, this is Captain Walter…"

"I know who he is," the judge said.

"Then you know that five hundred thousand is a ridiculous amount for bail," Harry said.

"Don't tell me what I know, councilor," the judge said. "Bail is set at a half million. Next case."

As the court officers whisked Walt away, Harry turned and looked at Elizabeth. "Would you come with me to talk to Walt?"

"We'll all go," I said.

"Are you family?" Harry asked.

"More than you'll ever know," Elizabeth said.

# Chapter Three

Walt sat next to Elizabeth at the table in the interrogation room at the county jail. I sat next to Harry.

Because of her status as County Sheriff, Jane waited outside.

"Before I can prepare an adequate defense, I need to know everything," Harry said. "Good or bad or indifferent, but everything."

"Oh, God help me if you're the best I can do," Walt said.

"Captain Grimes, insulting me is not going to help your case," Harry said.

"What fucking case?" Walt exploded. "There is no case, you twit. Don't you see this is a set up from the get-go?"

"It doesn't matter what I see or don't see," Harry said. "It matters what a grand jury sees. Now, where did the fifty thousand in your garage come from and the money in the Cayman Islands?"

"I don't know," Walt said.

"'I don't know' isn't good enough," Harry said. "The prosecutor is going to claim that you conspired with Jimmy DeMarko to import drugs into the U.S. and locally. That you took close to one million dollars as payment for allowing him such access, unimpeded."

"Oh, bullshit," Walt said. "Wire me to a polygraph and let me prove it."

"A polygraph isn't admissible in court," Harry said.

"But it holds weight with the newspapers and media," Walt said.

"I'll arrange it," Harry said. "Now I.A.D. has been working on this for months based on a tip from a C.I. that they refuse to give up. Would you have any idea who that C.I. might be?"

"No," Walt said. "I wouldn't."

"What's a C.I.?" Elizabeth said.

"Confidential Informant," Walt said. "And by the way, Jimmy DeMarko is dead."

"I'm well aware that DeMarko died of cancer three months ago," Harry said. "But their case against you is strong, Captain. Very strong. Circumstantial, but strong. We have a lot of work to do to prepare your defense."

"Look, I'm going to say this one more time, you nincompoop, I am being set up," Walt said. "By whom and for what reason, I have no goddamn idea. But I can tell you this much, find who set me up and why, or I'll never see the light of day."

"Captain Grimes, this is going to be a long haul," Harry said. "I suggest you ready yourself for that. Right now, I am meeting the district attorney in the judge's chambers and then I'll get back to you."

"Before you go, do you have a copy of the search warrant?" I said.

"Yes," Harry said.

"May I see it?" I said.

Harry opened his briefcase and dug out a copy of the warrant. I scanned it quickly. "The warrant is for the search of Walt's home, car and office," I said.

"That's right," Harry said.

"Walt's garage isn't attached to the house," I said. "It was added on later and is a totally separate building. The warrant doesn't cover the garage. I suggest you prepare a motion to suppress on the fifty thousand and present it to the judge. Of course, that's just a suggestion."

Harry looked at me.

"And see what you can do about bail," I said.

"Exactly what's your part in this, Mr. Bekker?" Harry said.

"I'm your second chair in Walt's defense," I said.

"Are you an attorney?" Harry said.

"You don't need to be an attorney to do the leg work, just a licensed private investigator, which I am," I said.

Harry looked at Walt. "Is that okay with you?"

"Jack is the best cop I've ever worked with, what do you think?" Walt said.

Harry sighed. "I'll be back after I see the judge," he said.

"Liz, I'll drive you home," I said.

I walked out with Harry and Elizabeth. In the hall, I said, "Harry, serve the motion to suppress the fifty thousand to the judge and then request a more lenient bail. And make sure the district attorney is aware I'm employed by Walt to act as your investigator."

I dug out a business card and gave it to Harry. "Call me on my cell phone when you leave the meeting," I said.

Jane met us in the hallway and walked to my car.

"I'll be back later," I told Jane. "Take care of Walt."

"Don't worry, Elizabeth," Jane said. "Walt is innocent. It will be proven in court."

Elizabeth nodded weakly.

Jane looked at me.

"See you in a bit," I said.

* * *

Elizabeth sighed heavily on the drive to her house. "None of this makes sense, Jack," she said. "I would know if Walt flew to the Cayman Islands, for Christ sake. His passport is expired, and I take care of all the bills. He would have had to pay for the ticket at the airport in cash and the hotel in Cayman, and never mind the fact I would have noticed he wasn't home."

I glanced at Elizabeth. She was starting to come apart, and who could blame her? After being a cop's wife for thirty years, just when Walt is about to pull the pin and retire, he's arrested and faces life in prison.

Instead of a retirement cruise, it's a courtroom, facing charges.

"What did they take from the house?" I said.

"Besides that box from the garage?" Elizabeth said. "Our computer. The checkbook and financial records, other stuff from Walt's desk, his cell phone and his guns."

13

"His car?"

"I don't know."

I turned down the block to Walt's home and swung into the driveway. The garage door was open and Walt's car was inside.

"I'll make a pot of coffee," Elizabeth said.

* * *

We sat at the kitchen table with mugs of coffee.

"We paid the mortgagee off two years ago, remember?" Elizabeth said.

"I remember," I said. "You had a barbeque to celebrate."

Elizabeth sipped from her cup and looked at me over the rim. "Do you think Walt did this?" she said.

"Not in a million years," I said.

"Who is Jimmy DeMarko?" Elizabeth said.

"He was a drug runner and button man for the Crist crime family," I said. "Walt tried to make a case against him for years. So did the feds, but nothing ever stuck. DeMarko got cancer and died about three months ago."

"Why do they think Walt had anything to do with this DeMarko?" Elizabeth said.

"We'll have to wait for the motion of discovery to find out," I said.

Elizabeth looked her question at me.

"When evidence is exchanged," I said.

There was a sudden rush of noise outside the house, and I went to the window to see what it was.

"Pack a bag, Liz," I said. "Those reporters are going to camp out on your doorstep otherwise."

"Where am I going?"

"My house."

"I can't do…"

"Pack," I said. "Or you won't be able to pick up the mail without fifty reporters following you to the door."

Elizabeth packed a large suitcase and twenty minutes later, we were seized upon by a horde of newspaper and television reporters. While they shouted questions at us, no one blocked our path to the car.

Then, as I opened the car door for Elizabeth, a reporter grabbed her arm. "Mrs. Grimes, can you…" he managed to say before I grabbed his arm, twisted it behind his back, and tossed him to the lawn.

Everybody shut up then, and I was allowed to get behind the wheel and drive away unscathed.

* * *

Regan rushed to the door when I walked in with Elizabeth's suitcase.

"Dad, it's all over the news," she said. She saw Elizabeth behind me and hugged her tightly for a moment. "How could they do this?"

"Regan," I said. "Go to my room and change the linen. Elizabeth is staying with us for a while."

Regan nodded and dashed off to my room.

"Liz, make yourself comfortable," I said.

"I don't know what to do," she said. She grabbed her suitcase. "I'll help Regan."

I went and sat down next to Oz on the sofa. He had muted the sound on the television, but the local news station was running the story on Walt.

"Is this shit for real?" Oz said.

"It's a set up," I said.

"They talking about some dead gangster Jimmy DeMarko," Oz said.

"I know. Turn it off for a while," I said.

"Liz sleeping in your room, where you gonna sleep?" Oz said.

"The daybed in the basement," I said. "But right now I have to get back to Walt."

"Should I dig out my old shotgun?" Oz said.

"Hell no," I said. "What's wrong with you?"

"You say that now," Oz said. "Sooner or later somebody show up with a gun."

"Make yourself useful and fix Elizabeth and Regan some lunch," I said.

Oz picked up his cell phone off the coffee table.

"What are you doing?" I said.

"Fixing lunch," Oz said.

"I mean in the kitchen," I said.

"You fix your way, I fix mine," Oz said. He held the phone to his ear. "Yeah, I'd like to order two large pizzas," he said.

# Chapter Four

On my way to the county jail, I stopped by Pat's Donut Shop and picked up four coffees and eight donuts. Harry called my cell phone, and I told him I would meet him in Jane's office.

While Harry, Jane and I waited in Jane's office for Walt to be transported from lockup to the interview room, we ate donuts and drank coffee.

Since Jane was responsible for Walt as a prisoner, there was no mention of Walt's case or Harry's meeting with the judge.

Jane munched her donuts, and then lit a cigarette as she sat behind her desk.

"You can't smoke in here," Harry said.

Jane blew a smoke ring at the ceiling. "I know," she said.

A deputy knocked on the door and then opened it. "Captain Grimes is in the interview room," he said.

"Play nice, you crazy kids," Jane said and blew another smoke ring.

As we followed the deputy, Harry said, "She's…"

"Yeah, she is," I said.

"She scares me," Harry said.

"Me, too."

Walt was wearing the clothes Elizabeth brought him in the shopping bag, but he needed a shave. I gave him the coffee and two donuts.

"So, let's hear it," he said, as he bit into a donut.

Harry opened his briefcase. "The judge agreed to the motion to suppress the fifty thousand found in the garage. He also reduced bail to two hundred and fifty thousand, but with the stipulation you wear an ankle monitor if you make bail."

Walt sipped some coffee and then said, "I'd have to put up my house to make that kind of bail."

"The case against you will be about the six hundred thousand in the Cayman Islands," Harry said. "The bank identified you out of a photo lineup presented by the FBI and the C.I. who tipped off Internal Affairs."

"Who is this C.I.?" Walt said.

"I'm going to have to subpoena him to appear at the grand jury," Harry said.

"So an unknown C.I. tips Internal Affairs that I've been working with Jimmy DeMarko to import drugs—who happens to be dead at the moment—and I've gone to Grand Cayman on an expired passport to hide six large and leave fifty large in my garage for anybody to find, is that about it?" Walt said.

"I admit it sounds comical on the surface, but there is no way around the six hundred thousand in your name in that Cayman bank," Harry said. "Even if we can discredit the C.I. who ties you to DeMarko, there is no way around that money. Unless you can explain it somehow that makes sense."

"I can't," Walt said. "Because it doesn't make sense."

Harry shook his head. "I'll be honest with you, Captain Grimes, I'm not good enough to win this case. You need Johnny Cochran or that guy in Vegas with the cowboy clothes. Somebody in that league, which I am not."

Walt sighed heavily. "My pension, if I collect it, is about sixty thousand a year," he said. "Before they seized our bank accounts, we had about fifty thousand in savings, and after putting our daughters through college, we're lucky to have that. How much would the guy in the cowboy clothes cost me?"

"His retainer is about two hundred thousand," Harry said. "Five hundred for a billable hour. Seven fifty for a courtroom hour."

"It's a good thing Jack works for free," Walt said.

"Harry, when do you get evidence?" I said.

"Sometime tomorrow," Harry said.

"Who is lead prosecutor?" I said.

"Tom Napier," Harry said. "And he's a total prick when he smells blood in the water."

"I know him," I said. "Call me when you have the evidence."

I stood up and looked at Walt.

Walt nodded.

"Where are you going?" Harry said.

"Don't do anything until I get back," I said.

I walked to the door, opened it and walked out.

* * *

"Where are you going?" Regan said as she watched me pack a bag.

"To get some help," I said.

"How long will you be gone?"

"Hopefully just one day."

I carried my bag to the living room where Oz and Elizabeth were on the sofa. Molly was on Oz's lap. Cuddles the pug was sleeping against Elizabeth's leg.

"Where you going?" Oz said.

"To try to get some help for Walt," I said. "Liz, try not to worry."

I looked at Regan. "No more pizzas for Oz, okay."

"I ain't eating no celery and carrot sticks," Oz said. "Or that hummus garbage."

"You'll eat what I tell you to eat," Regan snapped. "And you'll like it or next time you can do CPR on yourself."

Oz looked at me. "You going to let her talk to me like that?"

"Work it out while I'm gone," I said.

Oz looked at Regan. "Two out of three on Game of Thrones."

"Bring it, old man," Regan said.

# Chapter Five

I flew into Miami and then rented a car and drove to the Crist Mansion in Boca Raton.

It was close to nine in the evening when I arrived.

Eddie Crist, a powerful mobster, left half of his estate to his only daughter, Campbell, and the other half to charity.

Campbell's half was just north of a hundred million, plus the Boca mansion and the mansion back home, a dozen cars, and a private jet.

A few years ago, Crist helped me get sober when he hired me to find who murdered my wife. He'd always insisted it wasn't him, as I was investigating his crime family at the time. After my wife's murder, the case—and I—fell apart. Crist was responsible for putting me back together.

The top prosecutor at that time was Carly Simms. I'd known her for a number of years. She fell on hard times when she was accused of murder after a night of drinking. I helped find the real killer, and while doing so, I stashed her at the Crist mansion.

The next thing I knew, Carly and Campbell were an item. It surprised the hell out of me, and them, but who am I to judge people's happiness when it's in such short supply?

Since then, we've kept in touch, and I occasionally worked together with Carly, as she still practices law.

The gates of the mansion were locked up tight. An armed bodyguard was in the guardhouse, and he came out to talk to me behind the gate.

"John Bekker to see Miss Crist and Miss Simms," I said.

"It's after nine," he said.

"Call up, they'll see me," I said.

* * *

"Oh, look, Carly, it's a man," Campbell said, as she greeted me with a hug.

Campbell was around forty-two now, but still a knockout blonde. She took my hand and led me to the massive living room where Carly held a one-year-old baby girl on her lap. The baby was sucking from a glass bottle full of milk.

Carly looked at me. "The answer is no," she said.

"Oh, dear," Campbell said and sat beside Carly.

"I haven't asked anything yet," I said.

"That eighty-four-inch television on the wall there gets the same news as yours does," Carly said. "Walt is fucked and you're here for help. Is that your question?"

"Yes."

"The answer is still no," Carly said. "I have this diaper full of baby poop to worry about."

"We have two nannies," Campbell said.

Carly shot Campbell a look.

"Two nannies or twelve, the answer is still no," Carly said. She set the empty bottle on the coffee table, and put the baby over her right shoulder to burp.

"Walt helped you make a lot of good cases," I said.

"Walt is a cop. It's his job to make good cases," Carly said.

Campbell smirked at me. "Better try a new approach," she said. "Carly is in one of her bitchy moods."

"Call me a bitch again and I…" Carly said.

"Tom Napier," I said.

Carly snapped her head toward me. "What? What did you say?"

"I didn't call you a bitch," Campbell said. "I said you were in a bitchy mood."

"No, Bekker. What did *you* say?" Carly said.

"Tom Napier is prosecuting the case against Walt," I said.

Carly shook her head. "Napier is a…" Carly said.

"There is a difference, you know," Campbell said.

"What are you talking about?" Carly said.

"What are *you* talking about?" Campbell said.

"Ladies, you're giving me a headache," I said. "Can we please stick to one topic at a time?"

Carly handed the baby to Campbell. "She needs to be changed."

"Why give her to me? Give her to the nanny," Campbell said.

"At least take her to the nanny," Carly said.

Holding the baby at arm's length, Campbell left the living room.

"That prick Napier! About five years ago, he was my second chair on a murder case," Carly said. "He was more interested in getting between my legs than prosecuting the case."

"Your legs aside, Walt needs you," I said. "The public defender is way out of his league on this."

"Aren't they all," Carly said.

Campbell returned with a mug of coffee and handed it to me. "All she does is poop," she said.

"She's a baby," Carly said. "That's what they do."

"Why is it green?" Campbell said.

I sipped the coffee. It was good, really good.

Carly looked at Campbell. "I've decided to help Bekker help Walt."

"Like that was ever in doubt," Campbell said.

"Can we take the jet?" Carly said.

"Like I would ever be caught dead on a commercial airliner," Campbell said. "Bekker, we have something like a dozen bedrooms. Pick one and stay the night. I'll call the pilots and make arrangements."

Campbell left the room again.

"I'd love to nail that prick Napier," Carly said.

* * *

Sometime after eleven, I opened the French doors in my bedroom and stepped out to the large backyard gardens. I walked over to the pool and took a seat on a recliner.

It was a moonless night and the stars were visible in the sky.

The perfect setting for a cigarette, except that I promised Regan I would quit smoking, and I've done a decent job of sticking to it.

I heard soft footsteps behind me, and Campbell appeared and took the recliner to my left. She wore a thin robe over shorts and a tank top. Her long hair was down past her shoulders.

"It occurs to me that I never did thank you for giving my father peace," she said.

"It's the other way around," I said.

"Always the modest one," Campbell said.

She took out a pack of cigarettes from a pocket and lit one with a gold lighter. "I'm spoiled rotten, aren't I?" she said.

"There were times three years ago when I wanted to turn you over my knee and give you a good spanking," I said.

"Back then I might have enjoyed that," Campbell said and passed me the cigarette.

I took a hit. I said I was doing a *decent* job of quitting, not *perfect*. I held out the cigarette and Campbell took it back.

She reached out and took my hand.

"My father loved this place," she said.

"I can see why," I said.

We heard footsteps behind us, and Carly said, "If you two are having sex, I'm either going to shoot you dead or join in."

Wearing a robe over nothing, Carly took the recliner to my right.

"Baby Settina is hungry," Carly said. "I pawned her off on the nanny."

"I need a favor, a really big one," I said.

"Flying to Walt's rescue isn't enough?" Carly said.

"From Campbell," I said.

Campbell sighed. "How much is his bail?"

"Two fifty," I said.

"I'll post it," Campbell said. "But the next time *I* need a favor, you better come running on all fours."

"Agreed," I said.

"How are Regan and the old man?" Campbell said.

"Oz had a minor heart attack three months ago, but has made a full recovery," I said. "Regan is doing well."

"Good," Campbell.

From the house, the baby started to cry.

"Burp her, you idiot," Carly said.

"She knows to burp her," Campbell said.

The crying stopped.

"We take off at ten," Campbell said. "I suggest we get some sleep. We'll have breakfast on the plane."

# Chapter Six

The Leer Jet must have set Eddie Crist back twelve million or more. It seated ten and had a full kitchen, or galley, as it's called on a plane.

Besides Campbell, Carly, the baby and myself, the two nannies were on board. The nannies made us breakfast.

The nannies were very good cooks. I had perfectly made scrambled eggs, with bacon and hash brows, toast and coffee.

Campbell and Carly both had poached eggs with toast.

The baby had a bottle.

"So, tell me what you've managed to do so far?" Carly said.

"I got the judge to suppress the fifty thousand found in Walt's garage because the garage is a separate building from the house and wasn't covered on the warrant," I said. "I also got bail knocked down from five hundred thousand to two fifty, contingent on him wearing an ankle monitor and being confined to home."

"You've learned a few things from me, Bekker," Carly said. "Tell me what you know about the six hundred thousand."

"Working on a tip from a C.I., the Internal Affairs Division and the FBI teamed up to fly to the Cayman Islands where the bank identified Walt as having deposited six hundred thousand in a safe deposit box," I said.

"Oh dear, it sounds like Walt *is* fucked," Campbell said.

"Don't swear around the baby," Carly said.

"Settina is eleven months old, for God's sake," Campbell said. "She can't even speak yet."

"Well, when she does speak, I don't want her first word to be fuck," Carly said.

I bit into the toast and washed it down with coffee.

"Do we know who the C.I. is?" Carly said.

"No," I said.

"What about airline records of Walt flying to the Cayman Islands?" Carly said.

"None. Even the FBI doesn't have those," I said. "And also, Walt has an expired passport."

"Interesting," Carly said.

"What's so interesting about it?" Campbell said. "He could have flown under a different name for all we know."

"Interesting because it… why am I explaining this to you?" Carly said. "What about Jimmy DeMarko?"

"He's dead. Didn't you see the news?" Campbell said.

"I know he's… will you shut up?" Carly said. "Bekker, is there any proof or evidence that links Walt and DeMarko?"

"Just this C.I., as far as I know," I said. "I haven't seen any I.A. or FBI documents as yet."

"Did the department PB file a motion of discovery?" Carly said.

I nodded. "But I told him not to do anything until I get back."

"And who is the genius assigned?" Carly said.

"Harry Kane."

"I don't know him," Carly said. "He must be fairly new. Is he any good?"

"He admitted he isn't good enough to get an acquittal," I said.

Carly looked at me. "Do you believe Walt is innocent?"

"Yes."

"Why?"

"Because I know Walt," I said.

"That isn't good enough."

"Walt has been a cop for thirty years," I said. "If he was going to go dirty, do you think he'd be stupid enough to leave fifty grand in his garage and open an account in a foreign bank under his real name?"

"Bekker has a point," Campbell said.

"Shut up," Carly said.

"And the account was opened only six months ago," I said. "So, where's he been keeping six hundred thousand, in the garage? In a coffee can under the sink? Walt is much smarter than that."

"I'm sure they checked his bank accounts, phone records and computer," Carly said.

"Walt has his pension and fifty thousand in a joint savings account," I said.

"Not much for a life's work," Campbell said.

"He put two daughters through college and paid off his mortgage," I said, "on a cop's pay. That's no easy feat."

"First thing is get a discovery going on everything," Carly said.

A nanny came by with a pot of fresh coffee and filled all our cups. "There are fresh croissants if anyone cares for one," she said.

"I'll take one," I said.

The nanny brought me a croissant.

"Where do you think the six fifty came from?" Carly said.

"From whoever set Walt up," I said.

"Six hundred and fifty thousand is a lot to spend on revenge," Carly said.

"What makes you think it's about revenge?" Campbell said.

"Walt has sent a lot of people away," Carly said. "What better revenge than to send away the sender?"

"The name Jimmy DeMarko sounds familiar," Campbell said.

Carly rolled her eyes. "He was a button man and drug importer for your father, dear," she said.

"Well, that has nothing to do with me," Campbell said.

"I didn't say… never mind," Carly said.

I finished eating my croissant and washed it down with coffee.

Settina, on the lap of a nanny, started to cry. The other nanny got a bottle from the refrigerator in the galley and warmed it in a pan of hot water.

I looked out the window at some clouds.

"Napier, I.A. and the Feds are going to want to make an example of Walt," Carly said. "They'll want the maximum. Thirty years without parole."

I looked at Carly. "I know," I said.

"We have some work to do," Carly said.

"I know," I said.

The nanny fed the baby her bottle.

"While you're off having all this fun, what am I supposed to do?" Campbell said.

"Burp the baby," Carly said.

* * *

We landed at a private airport that caters to corporate jets. Campbell had made arrangements for two Uber cabs to meet us. One cab took Campbell, Settina and the nannies to her mansion.

Carly and I took the second cab to the county jail.

I used my cell phone to call Harry and asked him to meet us there.

"How *is* the bimbo?" Carly said after I hung up.

"If you mean Jane, she's fine," I said.

"Not what I meant," Carly said. "She's known Walt almost as long as you, and now she has to baby-sit him in her own jail."

"Jane is a professional," I said. "Friendship doesn't affect her judgment when it comes to her job."

"Let's hope so," Carly said. "Because she'll need to remain neutral at all times."

"She knows that," I said.

"Good. Now, we'll need a place to work," Carly said.

"What's wrong with Harry's office?" I said.

"They won't allow a hired attorney to work in the PD's office," Carly said. "I assume he's going to want to stay on as second chair?"

"Ask him when we get there," I said.

"We'll need an office," Carly said.

"I know just the place," I said.

# Chapter Seven

Harry Kane stared at Carly as if he hadn't eaten in a week and she was a juicy prime rib.

"Close your mouth, Harry, and tell me what you have so far," Carly said.

We were in the interview room awaiting a guard to deliver Walt.

"They won't…" Harry said.

"*They* who?" Carly said.

"Internal Affairs and the FBI," Harry said.

"Good. Now, what won't they?" Carly said.

"Internal Affairs and the FBI?" Harry said.

Carly looked at me. I shrugged. "Yes, Harry. What won't they?" she said.

"Reveal the identity of the informant who implicated Walt."

Carry scratched a note on a legal pad with a Montblanc pen. "Do we have discovery yet?" she said.

"They're dragging their feet," Harry said.

"What are they hiding?" Carly said. "If they've been working this case for months, then they should be prepared to turn over evidence."

"This C.I., who does he belong to?" Carly said.

"The FBI, I think, but I'm not sure since they won't provide any information," Harry said.

Carly looked at her Cartier watch. "Come on, Harry, let's go," she said.

"Where?"

"Courthouse to meet Campbell to make Walt's bail," Carly said.

"Bekker, tell Walt we'll be back."

"When?"

"Soon."

They left, and I waited for a few minutes until I grew restless and left the room to get coffee. I stopped by Jane's office but she was out. Down the hall there's a break room, and I went in and nodded to a few deputies at a table having coffee.

There was a coffee pot on a burner with coffee so old in it that I doubted it would pour, and there was a vending machine that, for a buck, gave you a fresh cup.

I sprung for two cups and carried them back to the interview room.

About ten minutes later, a guard ushered Walt in and removed his handcuffs.

"Not that I'm not always thrilled to see you, but where's the mope?" Walt said, as he took a chair opposite me.

I slid Walt's coffee across the table.

"I got Carly Simms as your primary defense attorney, and Campbell Crist is putting up your bail," I said. "Right about now, they're at the courthouse."

"A mobster's daughter is putting up my bail," Walt said. "How is that going to look, Jack?"

"Carly is putting up the bond and defending you pro bono, so don't worry about it," I said. "So you better be innocent."

Walt looked at me. "What does that mean?"

"No lawyers in the room," I said. "Just two old friends. As one old friend to another, is there anything to this?"

"How the fuck can you ask me that?" Walt said.

"Walt, for better or worse, I'm your ex-partner and your oldest friend, so I need to know," I said. "Is there anything to this?"

"I should get up and kick your ass," Walt said.

"You're better off drinking your coffee," I said.

"When can I see Elizabeth?" Walt said.

"Ask Carly when she gets back," I said.

"Goddamn it, Jack, when we find who did this, I'm going to lock him up for the rest of his miserable life," Walt said.

"First, you need an acquittal," I said.

Walt sipped his coffee. There was a knock on the door, and Jane entered with a paper bag and another coffee.

"I figured you wouldn't eat the slop we serve here, so I picked you up a couple of cheeseburgers," she said. "Medium greasy with bacon, just like you like them."

"There is a God," Walt said and tore into the first burger.

Jane sat on the edge of the table and looked at me. "So, I saw councilor Betty Boop and Harry the Hatless leave together. How did you manage to get her?"

"I asked," I said.

"And what did you have to promise in return?"

"Not a thing," I said.

Jane gave me her best suspicious look. "Uh-huh," she said.

Walt removed the second burger from the bag and tore into it.

"Stop by the house for dinner tonight," I said.

"Only if there's no talk of burger boy here," Jane said.

"I'll call you later," I said.

The door opened and Carly and Harry walked in.

"Right," Jane said. She stood up, nodded to Carly and Harry, and walked out.

"What did the Barbie Doll want?" Carly said.

"She brought me something to eat," Walt said.

Carly and Harry took chairs.

"Your bail has been posted," Carly said. "You can leave as soon as you put on the ankle bracelet. Harry?"

Harry opened his briefcase and removed the ankle monitor and set it on the table.

"All motion of discovery documents will be delivered by courier in the morning," Carly said.

"To where?" I said.

"The mansion, of course," Carly said.

I looked at her.

"What?" Carly said.

"With the baby and Campbell, the nannies and the bodyguards, and not to mention everybody knows it's the home of Eddie Crist," I said.

"I see your point," Carly said. "What do you suggest?"

"We use my trailer as an office," I said. "It's secluded, it has everything you need, and it's much closer to the courthouse."

"It's a dump," Carly said.

"When the press gets wind you're working out of the Crist mansion, how is a grand jury going to look at that?" I said.

"He has a point," Walt said.

"Harry, write this down," Carly said. "We'll need the following: a computer with a really good hard drive; a copy machine with a fax; a landline phone; a file cabinet, legal pads, lots and lots of pens and a few reams of paper. Give the list to Bekker."

Harry gave me the list.

"One more thing," I said. "It's impossible for Walt to go home. The press is already camped out at his doorstep."

"What do you suggest?" Carly said.

"A change of venue," I said. "Tell I.A. and the FBI he'll be confined to my house where Elizabeth is staying."

Carly looked at Walt. "Okay with you?"

Walt nodded.

"Harry, get Jane so she can put the ankle monitor on Walt," I said. "I'll take him to my place and then go shopping at the electronics store."

# Chapter Eight

"I'd forgotten how good a lawyer she is," Walt said.

"You couldn't afford her," I said.

"I can't afford you either," Walt said.

We were at a drive through at a Dunkin' Donuts, and the cashier handed me a tray with two containers of coffee. I gave her a ten spot and didn't wait for the change.

"I need some clothes," Walt said.

"Wear mine until Liz and I go to your house and get some," I said.

"A little big for me, aren't they?"

"That's the least of your worries," I said.

Walt opened his coffee and took a small sip. "I've done a lot of thinking the past two nights," he said. "Thirty years as a cop, and what do I have to show for it? A pension, fifty grand in the bank and not much else."

"You also took thousands of criminals off the streets and made this town a lot safer, put two daughters through college and paid off the mortgage, and you did it straight," I said. "Not many can say that."

"So you believe me then?"

"You wouldn't be in my car otherwise."

"So, where do I sleep?"

"With Elizabeth, of course," I said. "You're certainly not sleeping with me."

"I meant location."

"I know. My room," I said. "I have a daybed in the basement, but I'll probably spend a lot of time at the trailer before I lose it."

"I'm sorry about that, by the way," Walt said. "How long do you have?"

"The letter from the city gave me sixty days, so about fifty to go," I said. "Forty before they cut off the electricity."

"What are you and Oz going to do with them?" Walt said.

"Auction them off," I said. "Oz is taking care of that."

"Beachfront condos," Walt said. "That beach will never be the same."

"Nothing ever is," I said. "Including us."

I turned down my block and parked in my driveway.

Before we even got out of the car, Elizabeth opened the door and rushed out to greet us.

* * *

I did a turnaround with Regan in the car.

"Where are we going?" she said.

I dug out Carly's list and passed it to Regan.

"And all this stuff is for?" she said.

"Walt's lawyers, and you're going to help me set it up at the trailer," I said.

"It's going to cost you some burgers on the grill," Regan said.

"You're a cheap date," I said.

"You're a cheap dad," Regan said.

At the electronics store, Regan shopped while I pushed the cart. The tab for everything on the list was just over thirteen hundred dollars.

I paid with a credit card, the one that gives you reward points.

On the way to the trailer, we stopped at the grocery store and picked up what we needed.

I parked on the beach in front of the trailer, and we carried boxes and set them down outside the door.

"Dad," Regan said as she looked at the trailer.

"I know. Try not to think about it," I said.

I went in and carried out a large folding table and set it up. Then Regan went to work assembling things.

I went to work grilling burgers, a few dogs, and to toasting buns.

With everything half assembled, we broke for our very late lunch or early dinner, depending on your point of view.

By the time Regan had assembled and tested everything, the sun had set and we put everything into the trailer and sat in our old beach chairs to watch it glow over the ocean.

"Dad, isn't there something we can do to stop them?" Regan said.

"Like what?"

"I don't know, get a petition to the town."

"Two signatures don't make a petition," I said.

"I'll sign it," Regan said. "Father Thomas and all the nuns at the school will sign it."

"The school is in a different county," I said. "And a petition requires ten percent of the population of the town."

"So, they just take our trailer away and that's it?" Regan said.

"They're not taking it, they are buying our spot for twenty-five thousand."

"Even though you don't want to sell it," Regan said.

"It's the way things work sometimes," I said. "And besides, after we sell the trailer at an auction, we'll clear another fifteen thousand. That's a lot of college tuition."

We watched the setting sun and listened to the crashing waves for a few minutes.

Then Regan sighed and said, "Dad, is Uncle Walt going to jail?"

"Not if I can help it," I said.

"Be a good dad and see that he doesn't," Regan said.

"I'll do my best," I said. "Want to head home?"

"We are home," Regan said. "Let's stay the night."

"Okay. Give Oz a call while I change."

I went inside to my room and slipped into an old pair of grey sweats and sneakers. Regan was talking to Oz on her cell phone when I went out and around to the side of the trailer to work the heavy bag.

I warmed up with light jabs and hooks and then went to work and pounded the bag two thousand times before switching out to the speed bag for fifteen minutes or so.

I had a good sweat going and kept it going with sets of push-ups and pull-ups before returning to the heavy bag for another two thousand punches.

I ended with a hundred stomach crunches and a five-minute-long plank.

When I returned to the trailer, Regan was down at the water, sitting in the sand.

I sat beside her. We looked at the rising moon.

"What are you doing?" I said.

"Watching, listening to the waves," Regan said.

"I did that a lot," I said. "It got me through some pretty rough times."

"Condos on the beach," Regan said.

"Think of it from the town's point of view," I said. "It's millions into an economy that really needs it. The people that buy the condos put money into the town with their tax dollars, and they get a great place to live."

"And we lose," Regan said.

"Honey, it's the cycle of life," I said. "Do you know the one about the lion and the gazelle?"

Regan shook her head.

"The male lion is the top of the food chain and he loves to eat gazelle," I said. "The lowly gazelle is at the bottom of the food chain and only eats grass. One day the lion dies and his body fertilizes the grass the gazelle eats."

Regan looked at me. "Is that from some philosophy book you read?"

"No, the Lion King," I said.

Regan smiled. "Feel like a snack before bed?"

"Sure," I said. "As long as it's not grass."

# Chapter Nine

After breakfast, I went for a run at the water's edge, and when I returned, Regan, Harry and Carly were assembling things on the folding table.

A limo and driver were off to the side.

"Bekker, be a dear and get the discovery boxes from the car," Carly said.

I carried three large totes from the limo and set them on the table.

Carly looked down the beach at the waves. "Well, this is nice," she said.

"Is everything working?" I said.

"Fine," Carly said.

"Do you need the limo?" I said.

"Not for a while," Carly said.

"Can he give Regan a lift home?" I said.

"I don't see why the child can't ride in style," Carly said.

"I don't want to spoil her," I said.

Carly looked at the trailer. "Right," she said. "Regan, knock yourself out."

Regan walked to the limo and the driver opened a door for her. "Cool," Regan said, as she got in.

"So, what do we do first?" I said.

"Start by making a pot of coffee," Carly said.

I made a pot of coffee. Then I showered and changed and joined Carly and Harry at the table.

"Grab that folder marked credit card receipts and see what you see," Carly said.

I opened the thick folder. "It goes back five years," I said.

"It does, doesn't it?" Carly said.

I started reading bank-provided credit card statements. It was like reading the phone book. Seventy percent of the charges made were made by Elizabeth, and they were for clothing, sometimes household appliances, and the occasional dinner out. A few years ago, Walt splurged for a new hot water tank for the house. The rest of the charges were made by Walt's daughters, and they were mostly for college books and clothing.

One charge stood out like a sore thumb. A charge made four months ago at a jewelry store for three thousand dollars. It was made by Elizabeth.

I showed it to Carly. "Do we know what this is?" I said.

"No," Carly said.

"It's the only charge over a thousand in five years," I said.

I used my cell phone to call Oz.

"Regan home yet?" I said.

"Not yet," Oz said.

"Is Liz handy?"

"Hold on."

A few seconds later, Elizabeth came on the line. "Jack?" she said.

"A charge for three thousand made four months ago, do you know what it's for?" I said.

"Oh dear," Elizabeth said.

"What?"

"It's a retirement watch for Walt," Elizabeth said. "You won't tell him?"

"Nope. Thanks."

I hung up and reached for a folder marked phone activity. The FBI had pulled the landline phone records going back five years. The majority of the calls on the landline were made during the day, most likely by Elizabeth.

"Have they deemed any calls from the landline as suspicious?" I said.

"No," Carly said. "Every repeat number has been verified."

"What about his cell phone?" I said as I picked up the file marked cell phone records.

"No calls to or from DeMarko or any of his people," Carly said.

"What about statements from the C.I.?" I said.

Harry opened a tote and rummaged through it and handed me another thick file.

I glanced at a few pages. "The C.I.'s name has been blacked out," I said.

"We're meeting in the judge's chambers to request his identity be revealed," Carly said.

"What time?" I said.

"Three."

"Mind if I attend?"

"Have you a decent suit?"

"I'll get one," I said.

I called Regan on my cell phone.

"Dad?" she said.

"Is the limo driver still there?"

"He's having coffee and donuts with Oz and Uncle Walt," Regan said.

"Go to my closet and grab my grey suit, a white shirt, red tie, and black dress shoes, and give them to the driver to bring to me," I said.

"Sure," Regan said.

"Thanks honey. I'll see you later."

I set the phone aside and started to read. According to reports, the C.I. was on parole from a federal penitentiary and went to work for the FBI as an informant. Over the course of a year, the C.I. had been invaluable with the information he gathered on the streets.

Six months ago, the C.I. reported to the FBI that information learned on the street was that a police captain was in bed with mobster Jimmy DeMarko, allowing DeMarko free rein to conduct his illegal activities in exchange for compensation.

The FBI jumped on the information and asked the C.I. to get more. He did. Over the course of the next few months, the C.I. was able to narrow down the police captain to Walt, and that's when the FBI teamed with the state federal prosecutor and Internal Affairs to begin the investigation into Walt's involvement with mobster Jimmy DeMarko.

Dying from cancer at this time, DeMarko spent his final months in and out of a coma, and was of little use to the investigation.

After DeMarko's death, the C.I. brought in the golden nugget. He had information from a reliable source that Walt had a secret safe deposit box in a bank in the Cayman Islands.

With cooperation from the British and Cayman governments, the FBI flew to the island of Grand Cayman where the safe deposit box containing six hundred thousand dollars in Walt's name was discovered.

The bank manager picked Walt's photo out of a lineup, although he wasn't one hundred percent positive, as Walt had allegedly only been to the bank the one time.

The discovery in Grand Cayman led to federal and local warrants to raid Walt's home and arrest him.

I quit reading and set the files aside.

If it wasn't for the six hundred and fifty thousand, I would file it under "fiction."

*If* it wasn't for the six hundred and fifty thousand.

"Who wants some lunch?" I said.

Carly glanced at her watch. "We have time, what do you got?" she said.

"Burgers, dogs, steak tips, baked beans, and three different kinds of soft drinks," I said.

"Why not?" Carly said.

While I was grilling, the limo returned, and the driver carried over my suit.

I tossed a few extra burgers, dogs and tips on the grill, and we ate at the table with the sun on our faces and the crashing waves as background music.

After eating, I changed into my suit, and we took the limo to the courthouse.

As I looked around the plush interior of the limo, Carly said, "Welcome to the dark side, Bekker."

# Chapter Ten

The judge was a tough old bird named William Brooks. A thirty-year man on the bench, he had a reputation for fairness and toughness.

Tom Napier was surprised as hell to see Carly walk into the hearing room with Harry and me in tow.

"Carly," Napier said with genuine surprise in his voice.

"Tom," Carly responded, ice-water cold.

"Miss Simms, it's nice to see you practicing law again," Brooks said.

"Thank you, your honor," Carly said.

"Who is the big gentleman with you?" Brooks said.

"John Bekker, your honor," Carly said. "He's a private investigator retained for investigative purposes in this case."

Brooks looked at me, and then turned back to Carly.

"As I read in your motion, Miss Simms, you are requesting full disclosure concerning the identity of the confidential informant," Brooks said.

"Yes, your honor," Carly said. "As the People's case against Captain Grimes rests solely upon the shoulders of the informant, the defense must have the identity of its accuser to properly prepare our case."

Brooks looked at Napier.

"What say you, councilor?" Brooks said.

"Your honor, revealing the identity of the confidential informant will destroy his future usefulness to law enforcement, and might possibly put his life in danger," Napier said.

"Your honor, the defense said nothing about making the informant's identity public." Carly said. "The need to know speaks to his credibility as the only witness the People can provide. Their entire case against my client is this man's testimony, and we have the right to know who he is and how he came by his evidence."

"Your honor, please," Napier said. "Miss Simms is trying to overrule the informant's Fifth Amendment rights by…"

"Enough, Mr. Napier," Brooks said. "We both know the Fifth Amendment doesn't apply here. I see no reason why the informant can't take the stand at the grand jury hearing if I close it to the public."

"Your honor, defense requests the name and unedited reports submitted by the informant for the purpose of preparing a line of questioning at the grand jury hearing," Carly said.

"Granted," Brooks said. "Is there anything else?"

"No, your honor, not at this time," Carly said.

"Mr. Napier?"

"No, your honor."

"Then I will see you at the grand jury."

* * *

At the elevators, I pushed the call button and stood beside Harry.

Napier stood beside Carly, who looked at the closed elevator door.

"You're lucky the federal prosecutor isn't handling the grand jury," Napier said. "Once Grimes is indicted, the kid gloves come off. Once he's found guilty, the Feds will want their pound of flesh."

"Are you sure about that?" Carly said, still watching the doors.

"Sweetheart, it doesn't matter if you discredit my informant, you have no viable way of explaining the six hundred and fifty thousand," Napier said, "now, do you?"

"You always were too impressed with yourself, Tom," Carly said.

Napier looked Carly up and down. "Still got those gorgeous legs, sweetheart," he said with a sly grin.

The elevator arrived and the door opened. Napier took a step forward, and I reached out with my right foot, caught his ankle, and he fell into the car.

As the door closed, I said, "We'll catch the next one, *sweetheart.*"

Carly looked at me and grinned.

At the curb a few minutes later, Napier approached Carly from behind.

"I didn't appreciate your gorilla tripping me like that," he said.

I turned a bit and looked at him and he backed up a few steps.

"If I asked him to, he'd snap your neck like a dried twig," Carly said. "Now, be a good boy and send me the discovery on the C.I. like the judge told you to."

Napier turned and walked away.

The limo arrived, and we got in and rode back to the beach.

* * *

I pounded the heavy bag while Carly and Harry worked at the table.

Some of my best thinking was done while hitting the bag or on a long jog. The heightened activity pumped blood and oxygen to the brain, and after a while, I zoned out, and thoughts just seemed to free-fall and take shape.

After about thirty minutes of hard bag work, I pulled off the gloves and went around to the table.

"Is the cave man hungry?" Carly said as she looked up from a file.

"Where's that FBI report on the bank in Grand Cayman?" I said.

Harry reached into a tote and handed it to me.

"What's up?" Carly said.

I sat down. "Give me a minute," I said.

I flipped pages and read the FBI report several times. "The bank records show that the safe deposit box was rented six months ago on this date. The bank president and a few others looked at a photo lineup, and can say they are only seventy-five percent certain the man in the bank and in the photo is Walt."

"Seventy five percent is just good enough to sway a grand jury," Carly said. "Especially given the contents of the box."

"I know," I said. "But what I'm interested in is the date he opened the account. November 16th of last year. Get a warrant to search police department time records and see if Walt worked that day. If he did, he couldn't have flown to the Cayman Islands."

Carly and Harry looked at me.

"Harry, check to see how long it takes to fly to the Cayman Islands, and see if it can be done in one day," I said. "If Walt didn't work that day, could he have done a round-trip in one day and be at work the next?"

Carly picked up the landline phone and punched in a number.

"Judge Brooks, please," she said. After a few seconds, she said, "Judge Brooks, it's Carly Simms. I need to talk to you about another warrant."

Carly looked at me, and then said, "Yes, forty-five minutes. Thank you."

She hung up and said, "Jack, get changed. Harry, hold down the fort."

* * *

"Make it quick, Miss Simms," Brooks said. "I have a charity dinner tonight, and I'd like to go home and change."

"Yes, your honor," Carly said. "We can find no records in discovery that the work history for Captain Grimes was verified. We'd like to search those records to see if he worked on the day in question, when he was supposed to be in the Cayman Islands."

"The People didn't check those records?" Brooks said.

"If they did, they didn't include it in discovery," Carly said.

Brooks sighed. "You have your warrant, Miss Simms," he said. "But it pertains only to Captain Grimes. Understood?"

"Yes, your honor," Carly said.

* * *

"Three hours to the Cayman Islands," Harry said. "A few hours at the bank and make a quick turnaround, and it can be done in nine hours or so."

"But can you do it without being missed?" I said. "Grab the landline and cell records for that day."

Harry opened a file and spread documents across the table. "What was that date again?" he said.

"November 16th, last year," I said.

Harry used his finger to work down the list. "Three calls from the landline to his cell," he said. "And two from his cell to the landline."

"Time of calls," I said.

"To his cell at 10:20, five after one, and 2:40," Harry said. "From his cell to the landline at 10:43 and 2:56."

"Durations," I said.

"The shortest call was a minute and three seconds," Harry said. "The longest was two minutes and twelve."

"Do those sound like the calls of a man in the Cayman Islands?" I said.

"More like married couple chitchat," Harry said.

"Where are the passenger lists for flights to the Caymans on November 16th?" I said.

"We've gone over them a dozen times," Carly said. "If Walt was on a flight that day, he used a different name."

"I know," I said. I took the lists of the various airlines that had flights to the Cayman Islands on November 16th. "But fake drivers' licenses and passports don't grow on trees. An amateur, and even a professional, would choose a name similar to their real name to make it easier to remember. So, Harry, make a list of male passengers with the initials 'WG' and then run them down, and see if they're real people or not."

Harry looked at me.

"Go," I said. "Go, *go*."

Harry grabbed the lists, sat and got to work.

I looked at Carly. "When do you want to go to the station and serve the warrant?"

"In the morning," Carly said.

I glanced at my watch. "Grab the list of credit card charges for November 16th, and see what you see in that week leading up to that day."

Carly reached for the file as I went inside and made a pot of coffee. When I returned and filled our three empty cups, Harry said, "I have passengers with the initials WG."

"Harry, run down those names and make sure they are real people," I said.

Harry nodded.

Carly looked up at me as she grabbed her coffee mug. "The week of November 16th of last year, there is a charge the day of to an electrician. It doesn't say what it is, but that's easy enough to check."

"That's what the five chitchat calls were about," I said.

Carly's cell phone rang and she scooped it up. She listened for a moment and said, "Not much longer. See you in a bit."

She hung up and looked at me. "The wife wants me home," she said.

"What time do you want to serve the warrant?" I said.

"I'll pick you up at nine for breakfast, and then, right after," Carly said.

"Pick me up here," I said. "Take off, I'll put everything away."

# Chapter Eleven

I had dinner at home. Regan and Elizabeth made lasagna and some kind of Italian cake for dessert.

Walt and I took our cake and coffee into the backyard.

"Mind a few questions?" I said.

Walt looked tired and haggard, and who could blame him?

"Go ahead," he said.

"November 16th, the day you supposedly flew to the Caymans to deposit the money, there were five calls made between you and Elizabeth," I said.

"You're asking me about some calls between me and Elizabeth from six months ago?" Walt said.

"On that day, there is a credit card change to an electrician," I said.

Walt looked at me and then a light came on in his eyes and he said, "We had a ceiling fan installed in our bedroom. I remember now."

"Did you see the electrician?" I said.

"He showed up after I left for work," Walt said. "I think Liz called me around ten thirty to say he had arrived."

"It takes three hours to fly to Grand Cayman," I said. "The DA is going to make the case that you had plenty of time to make a round-trip and be home in time for dinner."

"Except that I didn't, and a passenger list will prove it," Walt said.

"They will argue you could have flown under an assumed name," I said.

"Oh, *please*," Walt said. "Even if I wanted a fake license and passport, I wouldn't know where to get one. I'd also need a matching credit card to pay for the plane ticket."

"It's doable, Walt. They also have a seventy-five-percent positive ID at the bank," I said.

"Yeah, from a six-month-old memory of someone they saw only once," Walt said. "That's bullshit and you know it."

I sipped some coffee and looked at Walt.

"I'm fucked, aren't I?" Walt said.

"Don't sell Carly short," I said. "It only takes one to hang a jury."

"A mistrial isn't the same as being found innocent," Walt said.

"First things first," I said. "Look, I got to go. We'll talk more tomorrow."

* * *

"How is Walt taking being babysat twenty-four-seven?" Jane said.

"About how you'd expect," I said.

"He's stir crazy without being in stir," Jane said.

She flipped off the sheet and reached for her cigarettes on the nightstand beside the bed. "I'm going to miss this dump," she said.

"Me too," I said.

"Want to go sit for a while?"

"Sure."

Jane slipped her robe on and I tossed on shorts and a T-shirt, and we went outside and took our old, rusty lawn chairs.

The moon was up and the tide was high and the waves crashed loudly on the sand.

Jane inhaled on the cigarette and blew smoke out through her nostrils. She was forty-seven now, but appeared a decade or more younger.

I told her so.

"That's because we're in the dark, silly," she said.

There was some firewood beside the large metal trashcan, and I tossed it in, splashed some lighter fuel from the grill onto it, and tossed in a match.

The fire glowed against Jane's face, and I had to admire what a gorgeous-looking woman she was, day or night.

"Ever think of making us permanent?" Jane said.

"Yes."

"And what do you think about that?"

"I think it's about time," I said.

"I've always wanted a nineteen-year-old stepdaughter and an old man for a stepson," Jane said.

"Then, I'm here to give you what you want," I said.

Jane inhaled on the cigarette and then blew a few smoke rings. "One thing we need to get straight right now, no more kids for me. I did my time in diaper hell, and I'm not looking for another go round."

"No argument here," I said.

"We'll talk about this more after you get Walt acquitted," Jane said.

I stood up and added another log to the fire.

Jane dropped her spent cigarette to the sand. "Let's go for a swim," she said.

Before I could object or agree, Jane was running down to the water. I jogged after her and by the time I caught up, she had tossed the robe aside and waded in up to her waist.

"I think skinny dipping is illegal," I said.

"I'll write myself a ticket," Jane said. "Are you coming in or do I have to drag you in?"

I removed my shorts and T-shirt and waded in up to my waist. "It's freezing," I said.

"Did it shrivel Jack's beanstalk?" Jane said.

She reached down and felt around. "Yup," she said, and then turned and dove under. She surfaced and looked at me. "Don't worry, I'll fix that condition later."

We swam around and rode the waves for a bit, and then returned to the trailer to dry off in front of the bonfire.

Jane lit a cigarette and passed it to me. "Sometimes I wish I could clone myself so I could go to work and still be a beach bum with you at the same time," she said. "But I guess it's impossible to be in two places at the same time."

I took a hit on the cigarette and passed it back to Jane. "Yeah, impossible," I said.

Jane tossed away the cigarette and stood up. "I'm cold," she said. "Let's go in and I'll see if I can fix that condition of yours."

* * *

Jane left for work around seven-thirty. I shaved, showered, put on a suit minus a tie, and waited in my lawn chair with a mug of coffee.

The limo arrived a few minutes before nine.

"It's impossible to be in two places at the same time," I said.

"Good morning to you, too," Carly said.

"We're not going to beat the six hundred found in the safe deposit box," I said. "Our best bet for a hung jury and a mistrial is to prove Walt couldn't be in two places at the same time."

Carly and Harry looked at me.

"Isn't that why we got the warrant we're about to serve?" Carly said.

"Yes, but I mean really nail it home," I said. "Last night I talked to Walt. Those five calls between him and Elizabeth on November 16th were about a ceiling fan they had installed in their bedroom. I looked through the checkbook statements this morning and Elizabeth paid the electrician by check."

Carly nodded. "A mistrial gives us added time to go for the acquittal," she said.

"It does," I said. "Where are we going for breakfast?"

* * *

The diner Harry suggested served excellent steak and eggs. The twelve-ounce steak was cooked medium rare, the three fried eggs runny over a bed of rice, the orange juice fresh and the coffee strong.

Carly had two poached eggs with toast, juice and coffee.

To my surprise, Harry had what I had.

"Napier is going to hammer home the point of the safe deposit box and seventy-five percent identification," I said. "We counter with it's impossible for Walt to be in Grand Cayman and working at home on the same day. Hammer the point home and one or two jury members will vote mistrial."

Harry nodded, ate a slice of steak and said, "And that buys us three months at least, if not more."

"How long will it take to prep Walt to take the stand?" I said.

"Not long," Carly said. "He's been on the stand hundreds of time before."

"Never as a defendant," I said.

"True," Carly said. "I can meet with him later today."

We finished breakfast, and I put the tab on the credit card I use for business expenses.

In the limo, I said, "Carly, you serve the warrant and let me take it from there. And tell the driver to stop at Pat's."

* * *

Carly served the warrant to the acting precinct commander.

He said, "I'd give you whatever you need to clear Walt without a warrant."

"I know, but it's better if it's official," Carly said.

We were in the lobby of the police station. Harry held three boxes of donuts.

"Bring one to the day room, one to the detective's squad room, and give me the third," I said. "Then meet us in the data room."

Sergeant Venus Brown, a beautiful black woman in her upper forties, was in command of the data room. Everything and anything pertaining to the precinct passed through her capable hands.

She stood from her desk and greeted me with a hug.

"Is that bribe in your hands for me?" she said.

"We have a warrant, so technically it's a gift and not a bribe," I said.

I set the box of donuts on a vacant desk.

"This is Carly Simms, Walt's attorney," I said.

Venus and Carly shook hands. "You used to be the D.A.," Venus said.

"In what seems like another lifetime ago." Carly said.

"So, what do you need?" Venus asked.

"Proof that Walt worked on November 16th of last year," I said.

"That's easy," Venus said. She went to a file cabinet and removed a thick logbook. "We still use a daybook around here."

Before computers and time clocks, most police precincts used a daybook where captains, lieutenants, and detectives would sign in and out whenever they entered or left the building.

Venus handed me the daybook and I flipped pages to November 16th.

Reading over my shoulder, Carly said, "Walt signed in at 8:45, out at noon, back in at one and out again just after six. He worked all day."

"Is this Walt's handwriting?" I said to Venus.

"You know it is," she said.

I looked at Carly. "We'll need an impartial handwriting expert," I said.

Carly nodded. "I know one," she said.

"Venus, we'll need all the paperwork Walt signed that day," I said. "Manpower reports, detectives reports, anything, everything."

Venus nodded. "I better get you a box," she said.

* * *

At the beach, we spread everything out on the table and read every document carefully.

"I know Walt's handwriting as well as my own and I have no doubt he signed all these documents on November 16th," I said.

"I'll call my expert and see if he's available for the grand jury," Carly said.

While Carly used the phone and Harry scribbled notes on a pad, I went inside the trailer and made a pot of coffee.

I brought it out along with three cups.

"He'll fly in for expenses only," Carly said. "He'll wave his usual fee of a thousand a day."

"Why?" I said.

"He owes me," Carly said and let it go at that.

"I checked handwriting in the day book, the manpower reports, sign offs on detectives reports, and if the expert can verify it as Captain Grimes's handwriting, our case to the grand jury is a strong one," Harry said.

"Did we get forensics on the fifty thousand and the cash in the safe deposit box?" I said.

"No. I'll give them a call," Carly said.

I drank a cup of coffee while Carly called the FBI lab.

"Not so much as a smudged thumb print of Walt's on the money," she said after hanging up.

"Let's go see a friend of mine who can help prep Walt for the grand jury," I said.

# Chapter Twelve

Frank Kagan answered his own front door and sighed when he saw it was me, Carly and Harry ringing his bell.

"Can we come in?" I said, as I walked past him.

"By all means," Kagan said. "Hello, Carly, who is your new pet?"

"Harry Kane from the public defender's office," Carly said.

Kagan caught up with me in his living room.

"This can only be about Captain Grimes," Kagan said.

Around sixty-five now with snowy white hair, Kagan was Eddie Crist's personal lawyer for thirty years.

"I need you to help prep Walt for the grand jury," I said.

"I'm semi retired," Kagan said.

"Seeing as how Eddie Crist was your only client, you've been semi retired for thirty years now," I said.

Kagan looked up at me and said, "Prep work isn't my strong suit."

"Aw, Frank, you've prepped hundreds of criminals for a grand jury. It's time you prepped a good guy," I said.

Kagan looked at Carly. "How is Campbell?" he said.

"I'll tell you on the way," Carly said.

"To where?" Kagan said.

* * *

Carly gave Kagan the details on the ride to my house. He scanned documents, asked a few questions and said, "How do you plan to beat the six hundred thousand in the safe deposit box?"

"We don't need to beat it," Carly said. "We just need reasonable doubt from a few jury members to get a dismissal and buy us some time before the Feds take control."

"Our handwriting expert will be able to tell if Walt's signature was forged at the bank in the Cayman Islands," I said.

"That's their entire case," Carly said.

"And it's a good one," Kagan said. "Do you have the identity of the C.I. as yet?"

"No, and that reminds me," Carly said.

She used her cell phone to call Napier.

When she hung up, she said, "It will be delivered tomorrow morning."

"And forensics on the money?" Kagan said.

"Waiting on results," Carly said.

"Straight out, do you believe Grimes is innocent?" Kagan said.

"No doubt," I said.

"The fix is in on this one, Frank," Carly said. "The only thing Walt is guilty of is being set up."

"Okay," Kagan said. He shook his head. "It will be nice to coach an innocent man for a change."

* * *

"My lawyer is married to the daughter of a mobster I tried to arrest, and now that same mobster's attorney is my jury coach," Walt said. "Who are you going to bring in next, Al Capone?"

"If he could get you a hung jury, I'd dig him up in a heartbeat," I said. "Now, are you going to give Kagan a hard time, or are you going to cooperate?"

Walt sighed loudly.

"Good," I said.

We were in my backyard at the patio table.

"But I won't like it," Walt said.

"You don't have to like it, you just have to *do* it," I said and stood up. I walked to the sliding door and tapped on the glass.

Carly slid the door open and she, Harry and Kagan stepped outside to the patio.

"Captain Grimes, nice to see you again," Kagan said.

"Councilor," Walt said.

Kagan, Carly and Harry took chairs at the table opposite Walt.

I stood in the background beside the sliding doors.

"You've been on the stand many times, but never as a defendant," Kagan said. "It's a different backyard when you're on the opposing side."

Walt nodded.

"So, let me explain something first," Kagan said. "Never take for granted that jury members are smart. Most aren't. The smart ones don't serve on a jury. And despite what they've been told by a judge not to decide by emotion, most do. If you come off as a cold, calculating prick, they will react to that. If you present yourself as a guilty-as-sin scumbag, they will react to that as well."

"All I know how to present myself as is me," Walt said.

"Understood, and I'm not here to change who you are, just to coach you on how to make the best impression on a jury, being who you are," Kagan said.

I ducked into the kitchen for a moment to grab some coffee and then returned to the patio.

"No big words," Kagan said. "Jury members won't be able to follow or remember big words. Short, concise, to-the-point answers. Look directly at the prosecutor when you answer and never at the jury. You don't ever want to appear as if you're looking for sympathy. Be polite but firm when you answer. Never sound like you're whining or angry or desperate. Don't say aspirate when you mean to say throw up. So, let's try a few questions."

Kagan turned to Carly and nodded.

"Captain Grimes, do you remember where you were last November 16th?" Carly said.

"At work, in my office at the police station," Walt said.

"That's more than six months ago, how can you be sure?" Carly said.

"I only remember because my wife and I had a ceiling fan installed in our bedroom that day, and she called me at work several times about the color," Walt said.

"She called you on your cell phone?" Carly said.

"Yes."

"So, you could have been anywhere when she called you."

"But I wasn't. I was in the office at my desk."

"How can you be sure of that?"

"I insist on having a log book at the front desk," Walt said. "We call it a daybook. For me, my officers, and detectives. Check the book. I signed in and out that day as I do every day I work."

Carly looked at Kagan and nodded.

"Captain Grimes, how do you explain the six hundred thousand dollars found in a safe deposit box in a bank in Grand Cayman?" Kagan said.

"I can't," Walt said.

"Can't or won't?" Kagan said.

"I can't explain it because I had no knowledge of it until I was arrested," Walt said.

"Even though witnesses place you at the bank and have a signature card that you signed," Kagan said.

"I've never been to the Cayman Islands, and my passport is expired," Walt said.

"Good. Very good," Kagan said.

I ducked back into the house where Elizabeth and Regan were preparing lunch and Oz was watching a movie on television.

I sat beside Oz.

"Got an offer on the trailers today," Oz said. "Fifteen thousand each. Plus the twenty-five from the buyout, we make out okay."

"Yeah," I said. "We do."

"Know what I was thinking?" Oz said.

"I'm sure you'll tell me," I said.

"We should take that eighty grand and buy us a three bedroom condo on the beach," Oz said.

I looked at Oz. "That's genius and that's exactly what we'll do,"

I said.

Regan poked her head into the living room. "Lunch," she said.

* * *

As we drove Kagan back to his home after lunch, Carly told him about the info from forensics.

"Not a useable print on the money found in the garage or the safe deposit box," she said.

"The prosecutor will argue gloves were worn," Kagan said. "And we still have no explanation as to the origin of the money."

"But we have enough to sway a jury member or two?" Carly said.

"Maybe. I'd like to work with Grimes a few more times," he said.

"Whenever you want," Carly said.

Kagan looked at Carly. "Any objections to me being third chair?"

"None," Carly said. "Harry?"

"None from me," Harry said.

Kagan looked at me. "Hey, I'm not even a chair at all," I said.

* * *

After dropping Kagan off at his home, the limo took us to the beach.

Carly and Harry made some notes while I made more coffee.

Around five o'clock, we packed up and called it a day.

Carly and Harry took off in the limo.

I sat with a mug of coffee and wrestled with my conscience for a while. If I had a pack of cigarettes, I would have lit one.

I didn't, so I changed and went for a jog on the beach with ankle weights instead. I timed the run for fifteen minutes and then turned around and headed back. I removed the ankle weights and sparred with the heavy bag for half an hour, and then switched out to the speed bag.

When I was done, I was soaking wet and ready to make a call I had no right to make, and one that would probably cost me a close friend I couldn't afford to lose.

# Chapter Thirteen

Paul Lawrence answered his cell phone while driving home in his car.

"I know why you're calling and the answer is no," Paul said.

I could hear traffic noise in the background. "I hope you're using hands free," I said.

"I am, and the answer is still no," Paul said.

"Paul, Walt gave you your shot," I said.

"I don't want to hear that, Jack," Paul said. "Not from you."

Back in the day, Walt, Paul, and I all were detectives, first grade. I made it to sergeant on a special organized crime task force before I imploded into a scotch bottle.

Walt stayed the course, made it to lieutenant, and finally captain.

Paul wanted the FBI, and it was Walt's recommendation that pushed him through and got him appointed.

"You don't want to hear it?" I said. "You're going to hear it anyway. Walt pushed you through when he didn't want to. Our department needed first class detectives and couldn't afford to lose you, but he did it anyway because it's what you wanted, not what he wanted. You're going to sit on your hands while he goes down, you selfish little prick?"

"Don't call me that, Jack. Come on, we've been friends too long," Paul said.

"Walt could do thirty. Is that what you want, Paul? Thirty for the man who got you into the FBI?"

"Of course not."

"Then are you going to help or not?" I said.

"You're asking me to interfere with a local FBI investigation," Paul said.

"I'm not," I said. "We're getting info on the C.I. who fingered Walt. All I'm asking for is a full profile on him."

Paul sighed. "I'll see what I can do," he said. "Call me when you have a name."

"Thanks, Paul. I'll call you as soon as I do," I said.

After Paul hung up, I called Regan and told her I'd be staying over at the trailer.

"How come you get to have all the fun?" she asked.

"We'll make a night of it tomorrow," I said.

Sometimes, what I do best is sit with a mug of coffee and think.

Even if we managed to get a hung jury, Walt was far from home free. The prosecutor would immediately file for a new grand jury, and the Feds could and probably would take over the case.

As I sipped my coffee, I thought about the money.

As a captain, Walt made around ninety thousand a year. Before that, as a lieutenant, around seventy a year. Detectives averaged low sixties.

Deduct around a third for taxes, pension, and health benefits, and there isn't much left at the end of each paycheck.

Toss in a couple of college tuitions, a new car every five years, and you wind up with exactly what Walt has, which is a livable pension and fifty thousand in the bank.

There is only one way for Walt to have accumulated six hundred and fifty thousand dollars.

The sun was starting to set over the ocean. The sky glowed and orange streaks glistened on the waves.

I took my car to town and grabbed a pizza and a large bottle of ginger ale, and ate in my chair facing the dark waves.

My mood was as dark as the sky.

To cops everywhere, I.A.D. were the vultures of the police department. They hung around like a dark cloud, waiting for a cop to pounce on like prey. The detectives assigned to I.A.D. were necessary to keep the police honest, but no cop is ever pleased to see them enter their house.

I went inside and sat at the table and dug out the I.A.D. reports. The C.I. on parole from a federal prison went to work for the FBI as a street informant and picked up information on a dirty captain in bed with Jimmy DeMarko.

*How did the C.I. pick up the information?*

Dirt on police captains didn't grow on trees or blow on the wind. And it was for certain that Jimmy DeMarko kept his business very close to the vest.

I searched through totes and read the reports filed by Internal Affairs Lieutenant Stanly Phelps.

Once the FBI brought the case to Phelps, I.A.D. dove into it like a swimming pool on a hot summer day. Phelps and the FBI flew to Grand Cayman to the bank.

It was Phelps who served the warrant and made the arrest on Walt.

I searched through page after page of reports filed at the FBI, I.A.D. and by the C.I., and "unnamed sources" were the words of the day.

Sending a career police officer to prison for life based upon unnamed sources didn't sit well with me.

A man had the right to face his accuser in court or out.

Around midnight, I stumbled into bed and went to sleep.

* * *

Carly, Harry and I were having breakfast at the diner in town before we went to work at the trailer.

A package arrived by courier a bit before ten.

It was the discovery information on the Confidential Informant.

His name was Ethan Jaden Smith. He was thirty-nine years old and spent half his adult life in one prison or another. His most recent stint was a three-year hitch on check and credit card fraud at Coleman, a medium security prison in Florida.

Since his release, Smith has acted as an informant for the local FBI and worked in a body shop in town.

He wasn't on parole, as he did every day of his three years.

How does a small time check forger wind up on the FBI payroll?

Carly and Harry got to work on a line of questioning for Smith at the grand jury hearing.

I changed and went to work on the heavy bag for a while. Then the speed bag, followed by sets of elevated push-ups, sit-ups, and then back to the heavy bag again.

Carly and Harry were still making notes when I put on the ankle weights and went for a run along the water.

"Hey, Bekker, let's do some lunch when you get back," Carly said.

I nodded and took off for the water. I jogged at a medium pace for about fifteen minutes and allowed my thoughts to freefall.

The whole thing stunk of corruption. How did a weasel like Smith burrow his way into the FBI's good graces?

Once, while waiting at the dentist's office, I read this magazine article by a famous writer. He was asked the difference between writing a novel and a screenplay. He said, when you write a novel you fill the page and when you write a screenplay there is a whole lot of white on the page.

Meaning, he left a whole lot of words out of a screenplay.

It flashed through my mind that the FBI and Phelps left a whole lot of white on the pages of their reports.

When I reached the midpoint of my jog, I stopped and removed the cell phone from my waistband and called Paul Lawrence on his cell number.

"Jack," Paul said.

"Ethan Jaden Smith," I said. "A check forger and credit card thief. His last stretch was three years at Coleman in Florida."

"That's a country club for non-violent offenders," Paul said.

"See what you can dig up on him for me," I said.

"Give me a day," Paul said. "And Jack, for what it's worth, I believe Walt is innocent."

"Thanks, Paul. Call me when you got something," I said.

I jogged back to the trailer and took a chair beside Carly.

"Frank Kagan called," she said. "He wants to coach Walt some more. I told him we'd pick him up for lunch."

"I'll grab a shower and change," I said.

* * *

Kagan read the file on Ethan Jaden Smith in the limo on the way to my house.

"What we need to know is what they left out of their reports," Kagan said.

Carly looked at me.

"Jack?" she said.

"I'll see what I can do," I said.

"Thanks for lunch by the way," Kagan said.

# Chapter Fourteen

Walt sipped coffee and looked at me.

"I never heard of Ethan Jaden Smith," he said. "Who is he?"

We were in the backyard at my house, seated at the patio table.

"He's the C.I. who fingered you to the FBI and I.A.," I said.

"I've never heard of the guy," Walt said. "Was he arrested through my house?"

"I don't know," I said. "I have Paul Lawrence looking into his background."

Walt took a sip of coffee. "I was wondering if you were going to give him a call," he said.

"Too much at stake not to," I said.

"Ask Venus to pull up the arrest record on this Smith and see if he came through my house," Walt said.

I nodded.

The kitchen sliding doors opened and Carly, Harry and Kagan walked out to the table.

"Are you ready for another session, Captain Grimes?" Kagan said.

"I'll see you later," I told Walt. "Carly, a moment."

She followed me into the kitchen.

"My car is back at the beach, mind if I borrow the limo for a bit?" I said.

"Go ahead," Carly said. "We'll be here for several hours, at least. Where are you going?"

"See Venus," I said.

Carly looked at me and then nodded. "No secrets on this one, Jack," she said.

"No secrets," I said. "You'll know when I know."

* * *

"He passed a dozen bad checks and ran up thousands in fraud credit card purchases before a store security guard pinched him passing a bad check at that big toy store at the mall," Venus said. "Two county sheriff deputies made the arrest. He pled out rather than face a trial and got three years at Coleman in Florida."

"Can I get a hard copy?" I said.

"Sure. Who is he?"

"Between us?" I said.

"Between us."

"The C.I. snitch who fingered Walt."

"This little punk?" Venus said. "It doesn't add up."

"No, it doesn't," I said. "I owe you lunch."

"And I'll let you owe me lunch," Venus said.

* * *

"Did you just arrive in a limo?" Jane said, as I entered her office.

"Belongs to Campbell Crist," I said. "It's Carly's wheels while she works Walt's case."

"I was just thinking of calling you for a little horizontal exercise," Jane said, as she lit a cigarette.

I took the chair opposite her desk. "One of these days you're going to set off the smoke alarm and have to explain to the fire department why it went off."

"I disabled the alarm in my office," Jane said. "What's that folder you're holding?"

I set it on the desk and slid it to Jane.

She picked it up, opened the folder, and asked, "Who is Ethan

Jaden Smith besides some punk arrested for check fraud?"

"The C.I. who fingered Walt," I said.

"This loser?"

"What do you have on him that's not in the report I got from Venus?" I said.

Jane worked her computer. "Not much," she said. "A career loser. Nothing I see that ties him to DeMarko, Walt, or the FBI."

"Can you get his present address?" I said.

Jane looked at me. "Don't go there, Jack," she said. "Walt is my friend, too, but violating the law won't help him."

"Who said anything about violating the law?" I said.

"Go home. Work out a bit. Take a shower, and wait for me to show up and get naked," Jane said.

"You're no fun when you're good," I said.

"I'm a lot of fun when I'm bad, and I'll be bad later," Jane said.

* * *

"How did Walt do?" I asked, as the driver navigated us back to the beach.

"If it wasn't for the unexplained money, he'd get a complete walk," Kagan said.

I handed Carly the file I got from Venus. She scanned it quickly and passed it to Kagan.

"The reports from the FBI and I.A. seem to have omitted a few details about Mr. Smith," she said.

"If you mean how a little twerp like Smith became an FBI informant, I agree," I said.

Kagan looked at me. "That would be nice to know," he said.

"It would, wouldn't it?" I said.

After we dropped Kagan off, we called it a day, and the limo took me back to the beach.

I changed and did a little bag work to kill time. By the time the sun set, I was on my third cup of coffee.

I was thinking about how nice a cigarette would taste when Paul

Lawrence called from Washington.

"This is not from me and I never called you," Paul said.

I looked down the beach and the approaching headlights.

"I'm not even here on my phone listening," I said.

"I dug as far down as it goes, Jack," Paul said. "We—and by 'we' I mean the FBI—usually keep meticulous records on informants and snitches, but not on this guy. Not on Ethan Jaden Smith."

I let that settle in for a few seconds.

"Jack?"

"I'm listening," I said.

"If there are detailed records on this Smith, I can't find them," Paul said. "It's not like a regional office to keep secrets, but on this one, they are."

"Who is the A.I.C. in the regional office?" I said.

"Don't do what I think you're going to do," Paul said.

"The names are listed online, Paul. How hard would it be for me to make a few clicks of my own?" I said.

The approaching headlights grew closer.

"Thomas Underwood," Paul said.

"Thanks Paul, you saved my fingers from undue clicking," I said.

"Jack, whenever you don't do what you're going to do, give me a heads up," Paul said.

"Goodnight, Paul," I said.

Jane's cruiser parked next to my clunker and her blonde head popped out. She looked at me and smiled.

"I need a shower," she said as she walked to me. "And that can go two ways. In the tiny, mold-infested shower inside that dump of yours, or are you up for another round of skinny dipping?"

"Skinny dipping still isn't legal on the beach," I said.

As she unbuttoned her shirt, Jane said, "I'll write myself a ticket."

# Chapter Fifteen

After Jane left for work, I took my chair with a mug of coffee and called Carly on my cell phone.

"Are you on your way in?" I said.

"As soon as I have breakfast," Carly said.

"Skip it and we'll have breakfast at the diner," I said. "We have a lot to talk about. And call Judge Brooks and request a pow wow with him for today."

"You've been busy, haven't you?" Carly said.

"See you in a bit," I said.

"Should I pick up Kagan?"

"Good idea," I said. "He'll want to hear this."

* * *

"So, the FBI and I.A. detectives have skimped on the information concerning this Smith character," Kagan said. "And you have that from a reliable source?"

"Yes," I said.

"We need to know more about Smith as part of Captain Grimes's defense," Kagan said.

"What did Brooks say when you called him?" I said.

"Fifteen minutes at eleven," Carly said.

* * *

Brooks received us in his office at the courthouse.

"What is it this time, councilor?" the judge said, as we stood before his desk.

"Your honor, the lack of information on the C.I. is making it very difficult for us to form a line of questioning," Carly said.

"I thought we covered this already," Brooks said.

"Yes, your honor, but the information presented by the FBI and I.A.D. is remedial, at best," Carly said.

She opened her briefcase and gave Brooks the files.

"No background information on Smith from either the FBI or I.A.," Carly said. "No reports on how contact was made between Smith and the FBI, how often they met, the C.I.'s sources, what he was paid for his information. Nothing, your honor. How can we prepare a line of questioning without the full disclosure?"

Brooks scanned the documents and then looked at Carly. "My conference room at two o'clock this afternoon," he said.

* * *

We had lunch at my house so Kagan could rehearse Walt some more.

"Jack, I really need some clothes and personal items from my house," Walt said. "Elizabeth, too."

"Make a list," I said. "Liz and I will take a ride over when we get back from the courthouse."

"The FBI and police usually pay for information," Kagan said. "They keep meticulous records of their meetings and payouts. My feeling is they have something damaging to their case they are hiding."

"Damaging how?" Carly said.

"What if they moved too quickly on the warrant? Or this Smith character isn't as reliable as they've made him out to be?" Kagan said. "Their case could be dismissed before it even reaches a grand jury."

Carly looked at Kagan.

"It won't cost anything to argue the fact," Kagan said.

"No. No, it wouldn't," Carly said.

* * *

Besides Napier, Lieutenant Stanly Phelps of the I.A.D. and Thomas Underwood of the FBI were present in Judge Brooks's conference room for the two o'clock meeting.

"Your honor, I formally protest this meeting," Underwood said.

"Noted. Now shut up," Brooks said. "I have read the discovery from the People to the defense, and I have to agree with the defense that it sorely lacks pertinent information necessary to form a line of questioning."

"Your honor…" Napier said.

"Be quiet, Mr. Napier, or I'll have you removed," Brooks said. "Now, I wasn't appointed by the president because I'm deaf, dumb and blind. Mr. Underwood, does the FBI generally deal with informants without keeping records of meetings and transactions?"

"No, your honor," Underwood said.

"Then, where are they?" Brooks said. "Lieutenant Phelps, I can say the same for you. You provided reports but no documentation to back up these reports. Do you have something to hide from the defense?"

"No, your honor," Phelps said.

"Lieutenant Phelps, Mr. Underwood, I want all documentation on my desk by nine tomorrow," Brooks said. "Disappoint me at your own peril, gentlemen."

* * *

In front of the courthouse, Carly and Napier squared off.

"It doesn't matter if you discredit my C.I. in court or not," Napier said. "You still have no way of explaining the six hundred large, and that will hang your captain by his thumbs."

"Are you sure about that?" Carly said. "Are you positive?"

Underwood and Phelps waited at the bottom of the courthouse

steps and I wandered down to them.

Phelps looked at me. He was of average height, a bit thick around the middle, and wore a suit several years out of style. "I'm thinking I know you," he said.

Walking down the stairs, Napier said, "That's John Bekker, Stan. He used to be Captain Grimes's partner back in the day."

"I was wondering where you fit in," Phelps said.

"Back in the day, if I did first-class-shit police work like you're doing, I wouldn't have made dog catcher," I said.

"Sing your bullshit all you want, Bekker, Grimes is going away for life," Phelps said. "And maybe we'll take a look at you, just for fun."

"I wouldn't push Bekker too far, you little runt," Carly said. "He squashes bugs like you before breakfast."

I turned and walked toward the limo.

"Yeah, well, he'll be Grimes's cellmate before this is over," Phelps said. "I remember you now and that messed up kid of yours."

I spun around, quick-stepped back to Phelps and was about to grab him by the jacket when Carly jumped between us.

"Phelps, you idiot," she said. "If Jack gets mad enough, even I can't stop him. Now give it a rest and back off."

I glared at Phelps. "Mention my daughter again and you will never mention anything again. Ever."

"Is that a threat?" Phelps said.

"No. A promise."

I turned and walked to the limo.

* * *

Kagan had his pants rolled up and his bare feet in the water. Harry stood behind him and talked to his office on his cell phone.

I had switched into swim trunks and stood next to Kagan.

"What do you think they're hiding?" Kagan said.

"Whatever it is has to be damning to their case against Walt," I said.

I waded into the water. The waves were low, the sun was high, and the water was warm. I dunked under and then stood in waist-deep water.

Behind Kagan, Carly appeared wearing one of Regan's bathing suits. It was a smudge too tight, but wearable.

For a forty-year-old woman who had a baby less than a year ago, she was in terrific shape.

"Campbell should be here with Settina in a few minutes," she said. "How is the water?"

"Warm," I said.

Carly gave me her Doubting Thomas face and dipped in a toe.

Harry put his cell phone away and dipped his bare feet into the water beside Kagan. "Judge Brooks wants to see us at eleven tomorrow morning," he said.

"Good," Kagan said. "We'll straighten a few things out."

Carly waded in a bit and then dove under. She came up opposite me and floated on her back.

"We need to shoot our load on a mistrial," she said. "They will re-file of course, but that buys us three months to work with."

In the background, the limo arrived and Campbell exited with Settina in her arms. She walked to the water and looked at us.

"How cozy," she said.

"Jealous?" Carly said.

"Of a man? Hardly," Campbell said.

"Water's warm," I said. "Put on a suit and take a dip."

Campbell stretched out her arms to me. "Hold this," she said.

I took Settina, and Campbell turned and marched back to the limo.

Carly grinned at me. "How long has it been since you've done that?" she said.

"Even if we get a mistrial and buy a few months, unless we can explain the six hundred thousand, the final outcome will not be good," Kagan said.

Carly stood up. "That's our ultimate goal, to find out where that money came from," she said.

"And how do we do that?" Kagan said.

Carly looked at me. "Bekker?"

"Someone has gone to a great deal of trouble to set Walt up," I said. "That same someone has suckered the FBI and Internal Affairs into believing it was Walt."

"Sure, but who is that someone and why?" Kagan said.

Settina peed through her diaper onto my chest and stomach.

"Give her to me," Carly said.

I passed off the baby, and dunked under and then stood up. "Do you need me tomorrow morning when you see Brooks?" I said.

"We can always fill you in," Carly said. "Why?"

"I have something to do," I said. "But right now, I promised Walt that I'd get him some clothes."

"We still have a lot to talk about," Kagan said.

"Fill me in tomorrow," I said and headed back to the trailer.

# Chapter Sixteen

**W**hile Elizabeth packed two suitcases for her and Walt, Regan and I sat in chairs in the backyard.

"This is so wrong what's happening to Uncle Walt," Regan said. "Last night I heard a noise in the backyard. I went to go see and it was Aunt Elizabeth crying to herself."

"This is rough on all of us, honey," I said. "And everybody is doing all that we can to help Walt."

"I know," Regan said. "It's just so unfair."

"A lot of things are unfair, honey," I said.

Regan looked at me and nodded.

"Let's see if Elizabeth is ready," I said.

* * *

Walt took a sip of coffee, set the cup on the patio table and said, "I'm going stir crazy, Jack, sitting around all day doing nothing like this."

"I'll see what I can do tomorrow," I said.

"This creep Smith was busted by Jane's department, so what's his beef with me?" Walt said.

"We don't know that he has one," I said.

"Well, he didn't pick me out of a hat like some damn rabbit," Walt said.

"Once we get a mistrial, we'll have more time to figure this out," I said. "Right now, there is someplace I have to be."

"Do me a favor and pick up some new video games," Walt said.

"Your kid whips my ass every time. Maybe a new game will give me a shot."

"I'll see what I can do about that, too," I said.

* * *

Venus lived in a nice townhouse on a quiet, tree-lined street in the suburbs. She answered the door when I rang the bell, and her face registered her surprise.

"Bekker?" she said.

"Got a minute for me?" I said.

"Come in," Venus said.

She led me to the kitchen, passing the living room on the way. Two of her four sons still lived at home. One was thirteen, the other eleven. They were doing homework at the coffee table.

"Boys, I have to speak with Detective Bekker for a few minutes," she said. "If I even hear a video game, I'll put the both of you in the microwave on high. Am I clear?"

In the kitchen, Venus filled two large mugs with coffee and gave me one.

"Let's go outside," she said.

Each townhouse had a walled-in backyard and a balcony on the second floor bedroom. We sat at the patio table where Venus kept her cigarettes and an ashtray. She lit one and said, "So, why the visit?"

"I need your help," I said.

"Little Miss Blondie should be scratching that itch," Venus said.

"It's about Walt," I said.

Venus blew a smoke ring. "No kidding," she said and passed me the cigarette.

I took a hit and passed it back.

"What I'm asking for is a matter of public record, but would take me a month to find on my own," I said.

"And what are you looking for?" Venus said.

"Cases that Walt was personally involved in where the suspect did time in Coleman in Florida," I said. "Say the last ten years."

Venus sighed.

"I know," I said. "It's a long shot, but this Smith character may have overlapped with someone in Coleman. It's worth a shot."

"Stop by around noon," Venus said. "Take me to lunch. Someplace expensive."

* * *

Regan tossed a log into the trashcan and red embers rose up and blew away on the ocean breeze.

She took a chair between me and Oz.

Oz sipped coffee.

So did I.

Regan drank soda from a can.

"The buyer for the trailer called today," Oz said. "His offer is up to thirty-five-thousand for the pair. What should I tell him?"

"Tell him forty and settle for thirty-seven," I said.

"Oz told me about the condos," Regan said. "Do you think it's possible we might get one?"

"Between what we get for the trailers and the buyout from the developer, it's very possible," I said.

"How's that grill going?" Oz said.

I got up to check. It was ready. I tossed on some burgers and steak tips and warmed up some baked potatoes.

"Make sure Oz's is well done," Regan said.

"Girl, you no fun at all," Oz said.

"If we get the condo, we won't have the beach to ourselves, but at least we'll still be able to do this as a family," Regan said.

I glanced at Oz. He had become so much a part of us that it was hard to imagine life without him.

Oz was the quiet to Regan's storm.

I flipped burgers and turned the tips.

"I call the man tomorrow and tell him forty," Oz said.

The dog and cat caught the scent of the grill and quit wrestling each other and came to my side.

"You'll get your swag," I told them.

Regan looked at me. "What's 'swag'?" she asked.

"Old people talk," Oz said. "Means your cut of the ill-gotten gains."

"Are you old, Dad?" Regan said.

"Ancient," I said. "Now who wants food?"

"Don't forget their *swag*," Regan said.

* * *

After driving Regan and Oz back to the house, I sat in the backyard with Oz, and we each sipped from a cold glass of milk.

The night was warm, the sky clear with millions of stars overhead.

"You know what I miss on a night like this?" Oz said.

"A tall glass of scotch over ice," I said.

"Read my mind," Oz said.

"You don't pass out and wake up with a freight train in your head from too much milk," I said.

"Everything have an upside," Oz said. "Even a glass of milk."

I finished the last few sips of my milk and stood up.

"I have to get going," I said. "Watch all the kids for me."

"Hey, Bekker, Walt gonna be alright. Right?" Oz said.

"Yeah," I said. "Walt gonna be alright."

# Chapter Seventeen

I went for an early run, and then worked the heavy and speed bags for about an hour. I took a cool down in my chair with a mug of coffee before hitting the shower.

While waiting to cool down, I called Jane on her cell phone.

"Feel like being bad?" I said.

"I'm only on my third cup of coffee, Jack. Ask me again around noon when my motor is running," Jane said.

"Not *that* kind of bad," I said.

"Is there another?"

"Later this afternoon, I'd like to run some things through the system," I said.

"By 'the' system, you mean mine?" Jane said.

"Correct."

"And by 'things' you mean names?"

"Also correct."

"And it has to do with Walt's defense?"

"Also, also correct."

"Make it late this afternoon so you can take me to dinner," Jane said. "A really expensive dinner."

"That might constitute a bribe," I said.

"Don't worry, I'll let myself off with a warning," Jane said.

"I'll see you around four," I said.

After getting off the phone with Jane, I had cooled down enough to grab a shower. I had one clean white shirt left to go with a tan summer suit. By the time I dressed, it was time to take a drive and see Venus.

* * *

"Is ten years enough?" Venus said.

"For a start," I said. "I doubt it's anything later than that."

"Well, let's get started," Venus said.

She checked records for arrests where the perp was sentenced to Coleman in Florida. After about an hour, the list contained sixty-four names.

We broke for the lunch I owed her as payment.

"What do you feel like?" I said, as we walked to my car.

"A nice bacon cheeseburger," Venus said.

"Sounds good. Where?"

"Christies," Venus said.

"Why am I not surprised?" I said.

"The devil gets his cut, Bekker. Always," Venus said. "You should know that by now."

"You need a reservation," I said.

"I know," Venus said.

Christies Steakhouse served a thirty-six-dollar cheeseburger. The burger was one pound of beef, six slices of bacon, covered in melted cheese, and served on a crusty club roll. A pound of seasoned fries and a bucket of cold slaw added to the fun.

Venus ate her burger with a knife and fork. I cut mine in half and ate it the old-fashioned way.

"When we get back, that number is going to double, maybe more," Venus said. "What do you plan to do with all those names?"

"I don't know yet," I said.

"Do you think one of these assholes is behind all this?"

I took a large bite of my thirty-six-dollar burger and shrugged.

"You're not very good at playing dumb, Bekker," Venus said.

"Who's playing?" I said.

"Do you know how unlikely it is for one of these scumbags to be behind this?" Venus said.

"Somewhere between very unlikely and impossible," I said.

"But you're going to try anyway."

"Wouldn't you?"

"I'd smack my head into a brick wall for Walt," Venus said.

"So, we're doing the same thing," I said.

"Minus the bloody nose," Venus said.

Neither of us had room for dessert, but we settled for coffee.

Then we headed back to the station, and Venus resumed work.

By three o'clock, she handed me a computer-generated list of one hundred and thirteen names.

"What are you going to do now?" Venus said.

"Homework."

"I have two little monsters at home that are good at homework if you get stuck," Venus said.

"I'll keep that in mind," I said. "And thank you."

* * *

I sat in my car and wished for a cigarette. When the urge passed, I called Carly.

"How did the meeting with Brooks go?" I said.

"Underwood and Phelps turned over their records on Smith to Brooks," Carly said. "Brooks is reading everything himself first, and wants to see us tomorrow morning at ten. Where are you?"

"Running down a lead," I said. "I'll tell you about it later."

"Harry and I want to do some work. How do we get into the trailer?" Carly said.

"Under the grill is a magnetic key holder," I said.

"We'll be around until six or so, will you be there?" Carly said.

"I'll let you know."

* * *

"A hundred and thirteen names?" Jane said.

"Only going back ten years," I said. "It could be more down the road."

I set the very thick file on Jane's desk.

"From Venus?" Jane said.

I nodded.

"She'd love to get her claws into you, you know," Jane said.

"She's helping me help Walt," I said. "Nothing more."

"Keep thinking that, and where do you want to start?" she said.

"Process of elimination first," I said. "Let's run through the list and remove anyone who is dead or back in prison."

Jane swung her chair around to face the computer on the table to her left. "Pull up a chair, big guy, this is gonna take a while," she said.

"A while" turned out to be three hours.

Of the one hundred and thirteen names, eleven had died and thirty-one were back in prison. Of the thirty-one, all had been arrested and sent back at least one year ago. The timeline eliminated them as suspects.

"That leaves seventy-one names to track down," Jane said. "What do you want to do next?"

"A complete bio on the remaining seventy-one," I said.

"You're talking *days*," Jane said.

"I know," I said. "We can at least start before we call it a day."

"You and I have different definitions of the word day," Jane said.

I looked at my watch. It was a few minutes past six. "Give me an hour and I'll take you to dinner," I said.

"My pick?"

"Your pick."

"Okay," Jane sighed, and went back to working her computer.

By seven, she had a complete bio on six names off the list.

"I can't promise you how many I can get to tomorrow, but I'll do my best," Jane said. "Now, let's get out of here, I'm starving."

"Where?"

"Christies. Know it?"

"You need a reservation."

"I know."

* * *

The woman at the reservations desk gave me an odd look, as she had seen me just seven hours earlier with Venus at lunch.

We were led to a cozy table for two in a corner beside a window. Jane ordered steak and I, still full of noontime beef, went with baked chicken.

"What do you plan to do with the six names I gave you?" Jane said.

"Read them."

"Any evidence as to who planted the money in Grand Cayman?" Jane said.

"No."

"So, how do the lawyers plan to beat this?"

"A dismissal to buy time," I said.

"Let me say that another way," Jane said. "How do *you* plan to beat this?"

"Turn over every rock I can think of until I find whoever is hiding under it," I said.

"Starting with those six rocks I printed out for you," Jane said.

"Police work is nothing but Point A to Point B, you know that," I said.

"Sometimes Point C gets in the way," Jane said.

"Is that your way of telling me to keep it honest?" I said.

"If you were still on the job and Walt was a stranger, how would you handle this if it came across your desk?" Jane asked. "Would the stranger get the same presumption of innocence as Walt is getting because he's your friend?"

"If you think otherwise, then the twenty years we've known each other has been a waste of time and energy," I said.

Jane looked at me and nodded. "Good boy," she said. "I think I'll check out the dessert menu, and no comments about my waistline."

* * *

I dropped Jane off at her cruiser. We made plans to spend the weekend together, and then I drove home to the trailer.

I made a bonfire in the trashcan as well as a pot of coffee, and took a mug and the six reports to my chair.

Before I settled in to read, I called Carly and asked her to pick me up on the way to see Judge Brooks in the morning.

Then I spent about two hours reading and rereading the six reports from Jane.

Two of the six were brothers and small-time bank robbers who served fifteen years of a twenty-year sentence. Both were arrested in the act by officers from Walt's house. Since their parole, they worked for the parks department driving garbage trucks around the parks.

Number three was a check forger who went down for the second time five years ago and served three years of a five-year stretch. He was busted by two of Walt's detectives. Since his parole, he's worked as a chef at the homeless shelter run by the Catholic Church.

Number four was busted in an FBI/DEA sting nine years ago that was started by Walt when he was still a lieutenant. He did every day of the seven-year sentence he received. He's fifty-seven years old and upon his release, he moved to Michigan to live with his daughter. He presently worked as the janitor in the apartment building he lives in with his daughter.

Number five was a lowlife mobster who exchanged information for a reduced sentence after being busted by Walt's detectives. After serving three of five years, he was relocated to an undisclosed location under a new identity.

Number six was a con artist type who flimflammed old ladies out of their social security checks and life savings. Walt was still a lieutenant in charge of the detective division when he arrested this genius.

I didn't bother to process all this information and tossed the files aside.

None of them had the resources to pull off something like what was done to Walt.

These were just ordinary, stupid criminals, as most were.

To do to Walt what was done required three things: brains, balls, and resources.

Some criminals had one of those, sometimes two, but to possess all three of those qualities was most unusual.

Almost unheard of, despite the super villains you see in the movies.

Around midnight, I headed inside and crawled into bed.

As I tossed and turned waiting for sleep, it occurred to me that Eddie Crist had all three qualities to take down a police captain and never did.

To a lesser degree, Jimmy DeMarko had the same qualities.

Both were hardened, career mobsters at the top of their food chain, but they also understood the rules of the life they had chosen.

In old Noir movies, the mob boss always swears revenge upon the copper that locked him up.

In real life, that was a line never crossed.

I finally fell asleep thinking I was looking for an entirely different animal.

# Chapter Eighteen

Judge Brooks received us in his office at the courthouse. Phelps, Underwood, and Napier sat in chairs on one side of the conference table, while Carly, Harry, Kagan and I occupied chairs on the opposite side.

Brooks looked at us all from his place at the head of the table. "I've read these logbooks carefully," he said. "The FBI and Internal Affairs Division have kept meticulous records on meetings held with Smith, how much he was paid, and the details of those meetings."

Brooks tapped the logbooks with his fingers. "But you know what I don't see?" he said. "References to Smith's sources of his information. In other words, his contacts."

"Your honor," Underwood said.

"Be quiet, Mr. Underwood," Brooks said. "Now, did you misunderstand me when I said to turn over everything?"

Underwood sighed. "May I speak?"

"By all means," Brooks said.

"Identities of informants need to be protected or we risk putting their lives in jeopardy," Underwood said. "If their lives are in danger, we will lose our informants, and they provide a valuable service to the FBI and police alike."

"I promise I won't tell a soul," Brooks said. "And neither will the defense."

"How can we be sure the information won't be leaked?" Napier said.

"I resent that," Carly said.

"I do, too," Brooks said.

"I apologize to the defense and to his honor, but the risk to any informant is high enough as it is without their names being made available to the public," Napier said.

"Your honor, we don't want to disclose any identity. But we do need to know the credibility of Mr. Smith's information," Carly said.

"I agree," Brooks said. "I'll have the names of Mr. Smith's street contacts by this afternoon. I'll decide then if they need to be made available to the defense."

* * *

Around five in the afternoon, just as I returned from a run, Jane called me on my cell phone.

"I have thirty more names for you, but if you want them you'll have to come get them. I'm stuck in the office," she said.

"I'll come get them," I said.

Carly and Harry were at the table. Carly looked at me. "Come get what?" she said.

"Something I'm working on," I said. "Call it a theory."

I grabbed a quick shower, changed, and drank a glass of orange juice before I left.

"How long are you staying?" I asked Carly.

"We're formatting a line of questioning for Smith," Carly said. "A little while longer, anyway."

"I won't be long," I said. "I can pick up a couple of pizzas on the way back."

Carly and Harry exchanged glances.

"From?" Carly said.

"Arthur's on Tremont Avenue," Harry said. "Brick oven. It's the best."

"I know it. What do you guys want for toppings?"

"Everything," Carly said.

"Call it in, and I'll pick it up on the way back," I said. "Wait about an hour and then call."

* * *

Jane met me out front and hopped into my car for a few minutes. She had a thick file folder and set it on my lap.

"My senior night deputy has the flu, so I'm pulling double duty," Jane said.

"We're still on for the weekend?" I said.

"He's either going to get well or die. Either way, we're still on," Jane said. "Right now I gotta go."

On the way back, I stopped by Arthur's and picked up the two pizzas and a bag of garlic rolls, and was back at the trailer before sunset.

Carly and Harry cleared the table while I made a bonfire in the trashcan.

Harry was a two-slice man. He stacked two slices together, folded them in the middle and went to town.

Carly ate hers with a knife and fork, while I followed Harry's lead and double stacked. There were a dozen garlic rolls in the bag, and we polished off all twelve of them.

"What are you up to, Bekker, with all this sneaking around?" Carly said.

"It's not sneaking if I tell you where I'm going," I said.

"But not what you're up to," Carly said.

"Looking for someone who has a motive for revenge," I said.

Carly glanced at the folder Jane gave me that I had set on the edge of the table. "In there?" she said.

"Possibly," I said.

"Do you need help?" Carly said.

"You have enough to do," I said.

The sun was about to set, and we watched it touch the horizon.

"Will you be available tomorrow?" Carly said.

"I don't think I need to be there to hear the judge's ruling," I said.

"We'll say goodnight then, and call you in the morning," Carly said.

After Carly and Harry left, I sat beside the bonfire and read the newest reports. I turned on the floodlight over the door to the trailer and read until midnight, and found not one damn thing worthwhile.

None of the thirty was exceptional and possessed the resources to set Walt up in such high fashion.

I was about to call Carly when I realized the time. It would keep until morning and so would I.

* * *

The sun rose as I jogged along the water. By the time I returned to the trailer, it was stretching high across the waves and heating the air.

I grabbed coffee, flopped in my chair, and called Carly.

"Change your mind about coming along?" she said.

"Nope. I'm going to pick up more reports," I said. "Meet me at the trailer when you're done with the judge."

"Lunch is on you seeing as how I'm working for free," Carly said.

"You're working for bragging rights over Napier," I said.

"True, but you're still buying lunch," Carly said.

After getting off the phone, I grabbed a quick shower, dressed, and drove to Pat's Donuts for a dozen to drop off to Jane's deputies.

"Not so fast, big boy," Jane said when I showed up with the donuts. "I'm claiming three of those."

I doled out three in exchange for a thick folder.

"The remaining thirty-five reports," Jane said. "I was bored last night."

"I'll make this up to you," I said as I tucked the file under my right arm.

"How?"

"I'll let the suspense work on you for a bit," I said.

"See you at the beach," Jane said.

* * *

I was reading the seventh report in the new stack when the limo arrived.

There was a fresh pot of coffee inside, and I brought it and three mugs to the table.

"How did it go?" I said as I poured.

"Brooks ordered Underwood to produce Smith's street contacts at the grand jury if we are not happy with Smith's cross," Carly said. "And by 'we' I mean the defense plus Brooks."

"Where's Kagan?" I said.

"We dropped him off to see Walt," Carly said.

"Where do you want to grab lunch?" I said.

"I saw an interesting shawarma place near the courthouse," Harry said.

"What is shawarma?" I said.

"I don't know, but it looked interesting," Harry said.

"Carly?" I said.

"Oh, why not," Carly said. "I could use some *interesting* today."

* * *

Shawarma turned out to be Middle Eastern wrap sandwiches made with chicken and beef that were actually pretty good.

As we ate, I said, "We need to go to Grand Cayman."

"Because?" Carly said.

"Because we have the right to interview the witnesses and determine if we want to subpoena them to testify at the grand jury," I said. "Is that *because* enough?"

"I think you just want another ride on Campbell's private jet," Carly said.

"It would be easier and faster," I said.

"Want me to call Campbell?" Carly said.

"Maybe it would be better if we asked her in person?" I said.

"I get to ride on a private jet?" Harry said.

We looked at Harry.

"Eat your shawarma," Carly said.

# Chapter Nineteen

"Are you out of your mind? Are you crazy?" Campbell said. "Do you know how much it costs to run the jet even for one flight?"

"Which doesn't matter when you just deduct it as a business expense," Carly said.

Campbell glared at her.

"I hate it when you're right," Campbell said.

"Call the pilots," Carly said. "I'll call the embassy in Grand Cayman and make arrangements for Monday and book a hotel."

"Our nannies don't have passports," Campbell said.

"Do we need them for a two-day layover?" Carly said.

"You won't need them because you will be working," Campbell said.

"We can take Regan," I said. "She got her passport last year, and she baby-sits for families in the neighborhood all the time."

Carly looked at Campbell. "Any more excuses?" she said.

Campbell sighed. "I'll call the pilots and tell them to register a flight plan," she said.

"I better call Kagan," Carly said.

"Is there anybody else you want to bring?" Campbell said. "It seats twelve."

"Don't be a bitch," Carly said. "Bekker, I think we're done for the day. I'll have the limo drop you and Harry off."

Carly walked Harry and me to the limo. Harry got in first. I waited for a few seconds with Carly.

"I'll call Kagan," she said. "Call me later and let us know if Regan wants to make the trip."

"What about Brooks?" I said.

"I'll call him and let him know," Carly said. "He won't object. It's part of the discovery process."

"I'll talk to you later," I said.

* * *

"I need to go to the mall to buy a new bikini," Regan said.

"What for?" I said.

"You can't expect me to baby-sit a baby by the pool or at the beach wearing the ratty old bikini I have now," Regan said. "Come on, Oz, we'll take my car."

"What for, I ain't wearing no bikini," Oz said as he stood up. Oz went everywhere Regan went and acted as her calming rod. Crowds still made her very uneasy, and Oz tended to bring her down a notch. "Maybe we can get some nacho fries at the mall?" he said.

"Maybe not. Let's go," Regan said.

After Oz and Regan left, Walt and I took coffee in the backyard.

"I don't know what to say, Jack," Walt said. "A whole lot of people are working on my behalf pro bono."

"Say thanks and move on," I said.

Elizabeth came out with slices of lemon cake that she and Regan had baked earlier.

"Thanks, hon," Walt said.

Elizabeth smiled and went inside.

We ate our lemon cake.

"Liz has gotten better in the kitchen since she's been staying here," Walt said. "She's picked up a few tricks from Regan and Oz. But I suppose I should get used to bad food where I'm going."

"The only place you're going is on a retirement cruise when this is over," I said. "And I have work to do, so I'll see you later."

Elizabeth walked me to my car.

"You're a good man, Jack," she said as she hugged me.

* * *

As I drove to the beach, I thought about what Elizabeth said.

A dozen years ago, after my wife's murder, after I dove head first into the bottle and abandoned Regan to a special hospital for traumatized children, would Elizabeth have said I was a good man?

We all pay for our sins one way or another. In this life or the next.

I had time and got in a quick workout on the bags, and then settled in to read some of Jane's reports. I read eleven and crossed eleven off the list, and quit reading when I spotted Jane's cruiser headed across the sand.

She parked beside my car, popped out like a whirlwind and said, "What do you want to do first?"

* * *

When our breathing returned to normal, Jane rolled off me and said, "Let's go for a dip."

"Moon's up and I saw a few people on the beach," I said.

"So we'll wear our suits," Jane said.

A few minutes later, we held hands as we walked down to the ocean. The tide wasn't up yet and the water was fairly warm as we worked our way into chest-high water.

"I'm going to Grand Cayman on Monday," I said.

Jane looked at me.

"To talk to the bank people that identified Walt," I said.

"Alone?"

"Carly, Harry and Kagan are going," I said. "And Campbell."

"Campbell?"

"It's her jet."

Jane's temper ignited faster than an eight cylinder Mustang. I could see it in her blue eyes as she squinted at me.

"What?" I said.

"Are you playing tic-tack-toe with these two averaged teenagers?" Jane said.

"What are you…?" I said, or tried to.

"Because I've had enough of cheating men to last me ten lifetimes," Jane said.

"May I remind you they are married to each other," I said.

"That doesn't mean they won't order from 'Column B' every once in a while," Jane said.

"Regan is going with us to baby-sit," I said.

That calmed her down a bit.

"Just don't tomcat around on me, that's all I ask," Jane said.

"I won't. I never have, and I won't," I said.

"You probably said that to Janet right before I stole you from her," Jane said.

"You didn't… she went back to her ex-husband, remember," I said.

"Let's go," Jane said as she took my hand.

"Where?"

"Back to bed," Jane said. "All this arguing has me in the mood again."

"Are all women nuts or am I just lucky?" I said.

* * *

On Saturday, Regan and Oz joined us for a cookout and an afternoon of swimming and sunbathing.

After I grilled us up some lunch, Regan and Jane went into the trailer and closed the door.

"Must be women talk," I said.

"It show time," Oz said.

"What's that mean?" I said.

"You'll see," Oz said.

The door to the trailer opened and Jane came out wearing a neon pink racing swimsuit.

"What's going on?" I said.

"You'll see. Regan?" Jane said.

Regan stepped out of the trailer and stood behind Jane.

"Now don't stroke out, Jack," Jane said and stepped aside.

I looked at Regan in her new, cobalt blue bikini that was basically a few pieces of string with a couple of patches of cloth.

I looked at Oz. "You let her buy that?"

"She paid for it with her own money," Oz said.

"*You let her buy that?*" I said again.

"She an adult now," Oz said.

I looked at Jane. "There's not enough material there to make a hankie," I said.

"She's almost twenty, Jack," Jane said. "It's about time she had some fun."

"Then why aren't you wearing it?" I said.

"Cause I ain't twenty," Jane said. "Come on, Regan, let's go for a swim."

As they walked past me, I glared at Oz.

"What? She *your* daughter," Oz said.

There was a group of young surfers sitting, floating on their boards. Jane led Regan past them and into the water. One by one, the surfers drifted closer to Regan and Jane.

"You see this?" I said. "This is your fault."

"What, it my fault boys like girls?" Oz said.

Several of the boys started talking to Regan.

"That's it," I said, and stood up.

"Bekker, sit your ass down," Oz said. "She come a long way since the home. She never gonna learn to talk to boys, and everybody else in the world for that matter, unless you leave her be and let her grow up."

I looked at Oz.

"As long as you up, get us some coffee," Oz said.

# Chapter Twenty

"First time on a private jet?" Campbell asked Regan.

With Settina sleeping in her arms, Regan said, "First time on a private *anything*."

Carly, Kagan, Harry and I were at the conference table. Carly made notes on a legal pad as they batted around ideas and suggestions.

"It all comes down to the money," Kagan said. "That's what they will focus on and we have no viable defense against it."

"If we get a dismissal at the grand jury, we'll have at least three months before the Feds convene a grand jury of their own," Carly said. "That buys us enough time to work on that and get ready."

Kagan looked at me. "Jack?"

"I haven't seen a report on the serial numbers of the money recovered in Walt's house or the bank," I said. "It might have come from a bank or armored car robbery for all we know. A motion of discovery on the recovered money might tell us where it came from and buy us a bit of extra time before the grand jury convenes."

Kagan, Carly and Harry stared at me.

"Just a suggestion," I said.

"I'll... uh... call Judge Brooks when we land and make the request," Carly said.

I glanced at Regan, who was feeding a bottle to Settina.

"Anybody want some coffee?" I said.

I went to the galley and put on a pot. While it brewed, Campbell joined me and rinsed the empty baby bottle in the sink.

"She's grown into quite the little lady," Campbell said.

"She's getting there," I said.

"How is she with the boys?" Campbell said.

"Shy," I said. "The cocoon she wrapped up in a dozen years ago has thick walls."

"Maybe Carly and I can help." Campbell said.

"How?"

"We were planning a vacation before you showed up looking for a handout," Campbell said.

"I wasn't looking for…"

"And once Carly is finished with this tawdry business, perhaps you would allow Regan to accompany us as our baby-sitter," Campbell said. "She'll work, earn some money, and visit some new and exciting places, not to mention mixing with all kinds of people."

I did the math quickly in my head. "She's very delicate," I said.

"I owe you, Bekker. My family caused what happened to her," Campbell said. "I'd consider it a favor to me if you allowed me to do this for her."

"When you have a quiet moment, mention it to her," I said. "I trust her to make her own decisions."

Campbell smiled. "Coffee is ready," she said.

I loaded a tray with four cups and the pot, took it to the table, and dolled out coffee to Carly, Harry and Kagan.

"When we land, a car will take us to the American Embassy where the chief of police will meet us," Carly said. "In the morning, we'll meet at the bank."

Regan was holding Settina in her arms, gently rocking her to sleep. "What do we do tonight?" she said.

Campbell smiled. "Relax, honey," she said. "We all *relax*."

* * *

Two cars met us at the airport. One car took Campbell, Regan and Settina to the hotel; the second went to the American Embassy.

The head of the Embassy was a diplomat named Burke. We took coffee in the embassy conference room.

"I understand you're just trying to present the best defense possible for your client, but it is a British Territory, so I must ask for your discretion in how this is handled," Burke said.

"We're not here to upset the tourist applecart," Kagan said. "We're just asking the same questions the FBI already asked and nothing more."

"I've spoken to the head of the Royal Cayman Islands Police Service, and an inspector will meet us at the bank in the morning," Burke said. "Just to keep things proper."

"Agreed, but we want no interference on their part," Carly said.

"As long as no British law is violated, there will be none," Burke said.

Carly nodded. "Then we will see you at nine tomorrow morning," she said.

* * *

While Carly, Campbell, Regan and Settina lounged poolside, Harry and Kagan went shopping downtown for cigars.

I hit the hotel gym.

They didn't have a heavy bag or a speed bag, but they had enough free weights and machines to keep me busy for an hour. Afterward, I ran along the beach for thirty minutes before returning to the hotel.

After a shower and change of clothes, I met the group in the hotel dining room for dinner.

Then came an early night.

Regan and I shared a suite, as did Carly, Campbell and Settina, while Harry and Kagan had private rooms.

Before turning in, I went to Kagan's room for a quick meeting. I told him what I wanted.

"I'm not sure that is entirely ethical," Kagan said.

"Of course it is," I said. "I did it all the time when I was a detective."

"Then why aren't you also telling Simms and Harry?" Kagan said.

"Harry is too green, and Carly, as good as she is doesn't have the poker face to pull it off," I said.

"Alright," Kagan said.

In the morning, we met for breakfast, and then a cab took Carly, Kagan, Harry and me to the bank.

* * *

Burke met us in front of the bank with the British inspector.

"This is Inspector Frazier of the Royal Cayman Islands Police," Burke said.

Frazier had a full British accent. "I'll allow you the same courtesy as your FBI in that I will not interfere, but I will not allow violation of our laws."

"We intend to violate none of your laws, inspector," Carly said. "Or ours, for that matter."

The bank president was around forty, wore an expensive suit, had perfectly cut hair, and if I didn't know he was a banker, I would have guessed his profession was undertaker.

His name was Cena and he was also British. We met in the bank's conference room.

"I have to admit I was a bit surprised to have to answer these questions all over again," Cena said.

"Different side of the aisle," Carly said.

Burke and Frazier opted to stand in the background and I joined them. I looked out a window while Carly and Kagan led the team.

"I understand it was you that opened the account for a safe deposit box for Mr. Grimes, is that correct?" Carly said.

"That is correct," Cena said.

"You met him, spoke with him, and checked all his identification?" Carly asked.

"Also correct," Cena said.

Carly looked at Kagan and nodded.

Kagan lifted his briefcase onto the table and snapped it open. He removed a file folder and opened it.

"This is a copy we obtained from the FBI of the signature card filled out by Mr. Grimes," Kagan said. "You identified it as his signature. Would you mind taking a look at it for us?"

Cena picked up the signature card and studied it for a moment. "That is my signature below Mr. Grimes's signature," he said.

"Are you positive this is Mr. Grimes's signature?" Kagan said.

Cena looked at the card a second time. "Yes, positive," he said. "I witnessed him sign the card myself."

"Thank you," Kagan said. He opened a second file. "This is the photo lineup the FBI showed you six months ago. Would you please look at it again?"

Cena looked at the lineup card.

"It's the same six faces," Kagan said. "Would you be able to identify Mr. Grimes a second time?"

"Certainly. Number four," Cena said.

"And you're positive?" Kagan said.

"Quite."

"Thank you," Kagan said. "Now, what is the procedure for putting things into and taking out of a safe deposit box?"

"A bank guard escorts the client into the deposit vault where the guard uses his key and the client his key to open the box," Cena said. "Both keys need to be inserted and turned at the same time. Then, the guard leaves until the client is finished."

"So no one actually saw Mr. Grimes put anything into the box?" Kagan said.

"Correct," Cena said.

"And without the client's key…?" Kagan said.

"The only way to open it would be to have a locksmith drill the box," Cena said.

"Will you be testifying for the prosecutor?" Kagan said.

"I've been subpoenaed," Cena said. "So yes, I will appear at the grand jury hearing."

Kagan nodded. "Thank you, Mr. Cena. We'll see you then."

* * *

The ride back to the hotel took just minutes. We met in my suite at the table in the living room.

"Well, Bekker, you were right," Kagan said.

I was pouring coffee into cups when Carly said, "Right about what?"

"Bekker substituted photo number four with a photo of his third cousin who lives in California and happens to look a great deal like Captain Grimes," Kagan said.

"What?" Carly said.

"That busts open Cena's testimony in court," Kagan said.

"And you didn't think to share this little nugget with me and Harry?" Carly said.

"Frank is used to lying with a straight face, you and Harry are not," I said.

Carly glared at me. Then she nodded. "I suppose that's a compliment of sorts," she said. "But don't do that again."

"So, who does the honors of throwing this brick at Cena in court?" Kagan said.

"You," Carly said. "Jack is right: you are probably the best at keeping a straight face while telling a bold-faced lie."

"Let's take the afternoon off and have lunch at the pool," I suggested.

"I don't have a bathing suit," Kagan said.

"Wear what you have," I said.

* * *

Carly wore a blue, one piece racing suit. Harry wore standard men's swim trunks. Kagan wore Bermuda shorts, a polo shirt and sandals.

I went with gym shorts and a grey T-shirt.

We ordered lunch poolside, and conversation centered on the line of questioning for Smith and Cena.

"Have you heard from Judge Brooks about identifying the

money?" I said.

"Not yet," Carly said. "But don't forget they're an hour behind us back home."

"Call him anyway," I said. "In case he forgot."

Carly nodded and took out her cell phone and made the call. She spoke for a few minutes and then hung up.

"He didn't forget," she said. "He's waiting on results."

"Good," I said. "Any idea where Campbell and my daughter are?"

Carly punched in another number on her phone, waited and then said, "Where are you?"

A moment later, she hung up. "Shopping," she said.

"I'll be in the gym," I said.

* * *

I was dressing after a shower when the phone in my bedroom rang.

"Bekker, drag your dumb ass to my suite," Campbell said.

"Because?" I said.

"Your baby ain't a baby no more," Campbell said and hung up.

I left my suite and walked down the hall to Campbell's suite where Carly sat on the sofa with a sleeping Settina on her lap.

Campbell held a glass of white wine as she stood beside the sofa.

"Where's Regan?" I said.

"Have a seat," Campbell said.

I sat next to Carly.

"Regan, dear, come show your caveman of a father what we picked up today," Campbell said.

The bedroom door opened and Regan walked out. It was a version of my daughter I had never before seen, and I wasn't sure I was ready for it.

She wore an expensive white pantsuit with matching high-heeled shoes. Her hair had been done professionally, as was her makeup.

She looked a decade older and reminded me very much of her mother.

"Spin," Campbell said.

Regan twirled and then looked at me. "Well?" she said.

"You're every bit as beautiful as your mother," I said.

Regan misted up as bit.

"Before we have a cry-fest, go change and show him the others," Campbell said.

Regan nodded and dashed back into the bedroom.

I looked at Campbell. "Thank you," I said.

"What's the point of being rich if you don't spend it once in a while?" Campbell said.

# Chapter Twenty-one

"How much time before the plane is scheduled to depart?" I asked Campbell over breakfast, poolside.

"Our flight plan is at two," Campbell said.

"I need earrings for Jane," I said.

"Because?" Campbell said.

"Because I like all my body parts right where they are," I said. "In one piece and connected to me."

"So, there is something you're afraid of after all," Campbell said. "If you'd like, I'll take you shopping."

"I can handle it," I said.

"Are you sure? Are you *positive*?" Campbell said.

I sighed. "No."

"I'll go with you," Campbell said.

The shopping district was a few blocks from the hotel. Row after row of jewelry stores lined two blocks, followed by boutique stores and a large tobacco shop.

"Anthony," Campbell said to a man behind a counter.

"Miss Crist, back so soon," Anthony said.

"My friend needs earrings for his lady friend," Campbell said.

"What is your lady friend's taste in earrings?" Anthony said.

"She's a shotgun-and-boots kind of girl," Campbell said.

I looked at Campbell. "That's not fair to…"

"Those will do nicely," Campbell said and pointed to a pair of diamond earrings under the counter.

"Excellent choice," Anthony said. "Would you care for a gift box and wrapping?"

"I'd care to know the price?" I said.

"Two thousand dollars American," Anthony said.

"That's a thousand an earlobe," I said.

"Wrap them, Anthony," Campbell said. "Bekker, hand over your credit card."

* * *

By seven o'clock, I was having dinner with Walt, Elizabeth, Oz and Regan in the dining room of my home.

Walt and I separated ourselves with coffee in the backyard where we could talk privately.

"How did it go?" Walt asked.

"The bank president is full of it," I said. I told Walt what Kagan and I did with the photo lineup card.

"I've met a thousand guys like him in my time," Walt said. "Willing to lie for their fifteen minutes of fame to jumpstart their career to the next level."

"I think he believes his identification," I said. "The question is why."

Walt sipped coffee and then sighed. "What are my odds?"

"For a dismissal? Even money at this point."

"In which case, the Feds take over and send in the big dogs at Justice," Walt said. "I can't beat this, can I?"

I wanted a cigarette, but drank some coffee instead. "Two ways to beat this," I said. "Find who set you up, or discredit all evidence and witnesses so the jury brings in a 'not guilty' based on insufficient evidence."

Walt nodded. "Which is Carly and company working on?" he said.

"Insufficient evidence," I said.

"And you?"

"Who set you up," I said.

"Is Carly and company aware of that?"

"I work better alone," I said. "But at some point, I'll make it known."

"Just don't make it the point where I'm being carted off to prison," Walt said.

I nodded. "Let's get back inside," I said. "I'll be sleeping here tonight."

* * *

After a restless night in the basement, I had breakfast early and was gone before eight o'clock.

Carly, Harry and Kagan met me at the beach around nine. The first thing Carly did was call Judge Brooks.

"Brooks said the FBI reports state that the six hundred thousand is untraceable," she said. "Not one serial number turned up on a hot sheet."

"What about the handwriting expert?" I said.

"We can't use the expert provided by the police or the one provided by the prosecutor or the FBI," Carly said. "We need an independent expert."

"Bill Tavers," Kagan said. "He owns a large security firm in New York. He's an expert at polygraphs, handwriting and interviewing. He's not cheap, but he owes me a favor or two."

"Call him," Carly said. "Set something up. I'll call Brooks back and add him to our witness list."

While they made calls, I went into the trailer to change. I emerged wearing grey sweats and T-shirt and immediately went to work on the heavy bag.

After fifteen minutes, I switched over to the speed bag, and fifteen minutes later to the jump rope, and then back to the heavy bag.

My thoughts were free-falling.

I knew Walt was innocent and there was a good chance of discrediting the witnesses, but the money was our Achilles heel. I left the heavy bag and did some elevated push-ups until my arms gave out.

Spent, I returned to my chair.

"The appointment with Tavers is set for noon tomorrow," Kagan said.

"Campbell is letting us use the jet, provided we don't break it," Carly said.

"What about the ruling on Smith's street contacts?" I said.

"He has until Friday to produce the names," Carly said.

"That's cutting it short, isn't?" I said. "The grand jury hearing is in two weeks."

"When we meet with Brooks on Friday, I can ask for a continuance," Carly said.

"Are you coming to New York tomorrow?" Kagan asked me.

"Sure," I said, stood, and went for a run along the beach.

"Our flight is scheduled for eight!" Carly shouted after me.

"I'll be ready," I said over my shoulder.

I jogged for about an hour. The feeling in my head was that I was missing something I should have seen by now.

Some overlooked detail.

When I was on the job and reached the point on a case where I was now, I would step back and give it a few days, and then go back with fresh eyes.

It was like watching a movie you'd seen before and noticed some little detail you overlooked, even if you'd seen it several times.

When I returned to the trailer, the gang was packing up for the day.

"We're calling it a day, Bekker," Carly said. "We'll need to be up early and fresh for tomorrow."

"I'll pick up breakfast on the way," I said.

After they left in the limo, I put on a fresh pot of coffee and grabbed a shower.

Then I took a cup to my chair, sipped, watched the beach, and thought.

Whatever I was missing or not seeing still escaped me.

Close to sunset, I spotted Jane's cruiser driving across the sand. It arrived and she got out, still in uniform.

"Got anything worthwhile eating in this dump?" Jane said.

"Nope," I said. "We can hit town or order out."

"Call the China Blossom and order one of everything," Jane said. "I'm gonna grab a shower."

While Jane took a shower, I drove my car to the edge of the beach where the public parking lot was located to wait for the delivery from the China Blossom. By the time he arrived and I returned to the trailer, Jane was out front in a chair, wearing a thin robe, and smoking a cigarette.

I set two large paper bags on the table.

"I got root beer, ginger ale, and Coke," I said.

"Root beer."

I brought out two bottles, plates and silverware.

We ate watching the sun sink lower in the sky. At dark, I made a bonfire in the trashcan.

"How was it hanging out with the Olson twins?" Jane said.

"That reminds me," I said. "I brought you back a little something."

I went into the trailer and returned with the little bag from the jewelry store on Grand Cayman.

Jane took the bag and removed the gift wrapped box. She looked at me. "It's not my birthday and it's certainly not Christmas," she said.

"It will be by the time you open it," I said.

Jane removed the gift wrap and opened the box. She removed one earring, looked at me and misted up a bit.

"Like it?" I said.

"Love it," Jane said. "You've made me very happy."

I shrugged. "Maybe you'd like to go inside and make me very happy?" I asked.

Jane stood and took my hand. "My pleasure," she said.

* * *


I woke up around two in the morning, untangled myself from Jane's legs, and stumbled to the kitchen.

I sat at the table with a glass of milk.

Jane woke up and, wearing nothing but her new earrings, came and sat on my lap. She placed her arms around my neck.

"I know this look," she said. "You're doing everything possible to help Walt."

"Am I?" I said. "So, why do I feel like I've missed something?"

"We all feel that way," Jane said. "It's in our cop DNA."

"Walt will have to spend the rest of his life in isolation if he's convicted," I said. "One day in the yard and he's done. That's some reward for thirty years on the job."

"Jack, you can only do what you can do," Jane said. "And seeing as how you have an early date with the Olson Twins, come back to bed and get some sleep."

Jane stood up and took my hand. "I got just the thing that will make you sleep like a baby," she said.

And she was right.

# Chapter Twenty-two

We landed at a small, private airport in the borough of Queens and took an Uber cab to Manhattan.

Bill Tavers had a large office on 45th Street and Park Avenue. He was around Kagan's age, slim, and wore a beard to offset his receding hairline.

Kagan made the introductions. Then we met in a large conference room.

"I employ three polygraph technicians, three investigators and two forensic specialists," Tavers said. "I myself was a foremost handwriting expert for the department for twenty-five years."

Kagan opened his briefcase and removed a folder and set it on the table. He removed several documents.

"These are samples of the signature of Captain Walter Grimes," Kagan said.

Tavers studied the signatures for several moments.

Kagan produced a copy of the signature card from the Cayman bank.

"The original?" Tavers said.

"Unavailable," Kagan said.

"Then I can give you only a partial decision," Tavers said. "I can't judge the depth on the card to the depth on the documents without the original."

"Understood," Kagan said.

Tavers studied the signatures carefully, using a magnifying glass and finally said, "The documents are consistent with how much pressure Grimes uses when signing his name. That information is missing from the bank card."

"And the rest?" Kagan said.

"Whoever signed the card was good. Damn good," Tavers said. "But it wasn't signed by Grimes."

"Are you sure enough to write a statement?" Kagan said.

"I'll appear in court if you want and explain the report and my findings," Tavers said. "I'll wave my usual fee except for plane fare and a hotel."

"That is what I was hoping you would say," Kagan said.

"I'm John Bekker," I said.

"I know who you are," Tavers said. "That was a hell of a job you did in Puerto Rico last year."

"Thanks," I said. "So, in your expert opinion, how difficult would it be to forge Walt Grimes's signature?"

"It's difficult to forge anybody's signature and make it pass," Tavers said.

"So this individual had to practice it?" I said.

"A great deal," Tavers said. "This signature required a lot of skill, and that means you're dealing with someone highly intelligent. It's no accident that the forged signature is detectable to a very few, and even then, it would fool some of the best."

"Like the FBI and local police?" I said.

"I'll take the Pepsi challenge against the FBI any day of the week," Tavers said.

"In court, you just might," I said.

Tavers nodded. "Looking forward to it," he said.

"So, Bill, would you care to join us for lunch? Kagan asked.

* * *

We ate at a large Mexican restaurant a few blocks from Tavers's office. Once we settled in and ordered, Tavers said, "So, Jack, that job you did in Puerto Rico was first rate. Congratulations."

"Thanks, but I had a lot of help," I said.

"I'm tired of losing business in your neck of the woods, Jack," Tavers said. "I could use someone with your skill. You'd still be independent, but partnered with my firm, you'd have a lot more resources."

"Give me some time to wrap this up and I'll get back to you," I said. "We can talk about it in a few months, if that's okay with you."

"Sounds good," Tavers said. "Frank, my report will be in the mail tomorrow."

* * *

"We can discredit the signature card and photo lineup, but is that enough at this point?" Kagan said.

I was drinking coffee and watching clouds below us as we flew home.

"My opinion is we need to somehow discredit the safe deposit box," Carly said.

"Harry?" Kagan said.

"I agree," Harry said. "I've been putting myself in Napier's shoes, and my plan of attack would be the money and this Smith character. I don't see how we can overcome those two things."

"Bekker?" Kagan said.

"The goal is a dismissal to buy some time, so focus on that," I said. "Work the jury, milk their emotions. Gain the sympathy of one or two of them. We'll get a mistrial based on emotion. Napier has to know we'll go that route, but what's he going to counter it with?"

"Facts," Harry said.

"True, but what exactly are the facts?" I said. "They can't physically prove Walt was in Grand Cayman. The cameras in the bank are set up to record and hold for thirty days, so video evidence is gone. The same is true for the airport. The fifty thousand found in the garage is out. We can discredit the handwriting on the bank signature card and discredit the photo lineup. Their star witness is this Smith guy, and he's shaky at best, not to mention his street informants that we still don't know about. There is no record of Walt's passport being

112

updated or a flight that he was scheduled on. The only real fact left is the six hundred thousand found in the safe deposit box."

"Which, we can't refute," Carly said.

"We don't have to in order to get a few of the grand jury members to see it our way," I said. "You and Frank milk it, butter it, wrap it in sweet cream if you have to, but gain some sympathy for Walt and we have our dismissal."

Carly, Frank and Harry looked at me.

"I can see why you were the only one to ever get close to Eddie Crist," Kagan said.

* * *

I went for a jog along the beach and returned to the trailer in time to watch the sunset.

Tomorrow morning, we would meet with Judge Brooks to discuss Smith's street informants at eleven.

I could have gone home for the night, but I preferred my own company when think-time was required.

I made a fire in the trashcan and drank coffee.

How do you account for six hundred thousand dollars?

Walt certainly didn't save it from his salary. He didn't borrow it from a bank or a loan shark. He didn't inherit it from a long-lost relative or win the lottery.

Other than Smith's word that the money came from Jimmy DeMarko, there was no evidence that it actually did.

I grabbed my cell phone and called Kagan.

"Frank, it's Bekker," I said when he answered.

"Is something wrong?" Kagan said.

"Just thinking about something," I said. "Who took DeMarko's place after he died?"

"Tony Rizzo. Why?"

"Can you get me in to see him?"

After a short pause, Kagan said, "Because?"

"Some things are best heard directly from the horse's mouth,"

I said.

"I'll make a call," Kagan said.

"Thanks."

"See you in the morning," Kagan said.

"Good night, Frank," I said.

I set the phone aside and watched the bonfire in the trashcan start to burn down.

"Tony Rizzo," I said aloud.

# Chapter Twenty-three

"I find the list of street informants for Smith to be sketchy at best," Judge Brooks said. "It reads like a book of 'he said, she said.' However, I will allow them to be called to the stand and crossed by the defense if they want the opportunity."

"Copies of reports to study for cross," Carly said.

"Noted," Brooks said. "Pick them up on the way out."

* * *

On the courthouse steps, Kagan said, "Bekker and I have a brief appointment."

"I was wondering why you took your own car," Carly said.

"See you back at the ranch," I said.

Kagan drove a two-year-old Cadillac that rode like a boat on smooth water.

The drive took about forty-five-minutes. Rizzo lived in a nice, if modest, home in the suburbs. It was surrounded by a stone wall with access through a gate.

"Frank Kagan and John Bekker to see Mr. Rizzo," Kagan told the bodyguard manning the fence.

* * *

"Something to drink?" Rizzo said when Kagan and I took chairs in the study.

"Coffee," I said.

Rizzo looked past us to the bodyguard against the wall. "Three espressos," he said, and the bodyguard left us to fetch them.

"So, Frank, you said you had some questions about Jimmy," Rizzo said.

Rizzo was around sixty, slender, with graying hair and brown eyes. He was ordinary looking except for his eyes. Any high-ranking mobster anywhere has that look in his eyes. A look that says danger.

If you put a diamondback rattler next to a harmless garden snake and just saw the eyes of both, you'd know which one to avoid.

It was that way with mobsters.

"My associate John Bekker actually is the one who wanted to speak with you, Tony," Kagan said.

Rizzo shifted his eyes over to me. "I haven't had the pleasure, but I know who you are by reputation," he said.

The door opened and the bodyguard returned with a tray that held three small cups of espresso. He set the cups in front of us, turned, and took his place against the wall.

"So, John Bekker, what do you want to speak to me about?" Rizzo said.

"Jimmy DeMarko," I said.

Rizzo sipped some of his coffee. "Sadly, Jimmy passed away," he said.

"I'm aware of that," I said. I sampled the espresso. "This might be the best coffee I've ever tasted."

"I have a coffee machine in the kitchen made of brass," Rizzo said. "It makes regular, espresso, cappuccino. Cost nine thousand. So, what do you want to know about Jimmy?"

"Are you aware of the situation involving Police Captain Walt Grimes?" I said.

Rizzo sipped more coffee. So did I.

"Do you think I live in a bubble?" Rizzo said.

"Is it true?" I said.

Rizzo measured his words carefully. "This isn't the forties or even the seventies, Mr. Bekker, where we needed police captains and judges on our payroll to do business," he said. We're not shooting each other in the streets of Manhattan in power wars anymore. We have investment bankers who run things for us. We own businesses countrywide and overseas, and do business with foreign governments and even our own. The notion that Jimmy would feel the need to bribe a police captain to let him operate locally is laughable to me."

"So, you don't believe Jimmy DeMarko paid Captain Grimes to look the other way and allow him to do business?" I said.

"I just said that," Rizzo said.

"How do you explain the confidential informant?" I said.

"Mr. Bekker, if by some miracle some police snitch stumbled upon any information regarding anything to do with our business, that snitch would have disappeared long before he got the chance to use it," Rizzo said. "We place a premium on our privacy, and the last thing we tolerate is publicity. No, your police captain is the victim of a set-up, and Jimmy was chosen because it was known he wouldn't be around to defend himself or indict."

"About how I see things, too," I said.

"Captain Grimes is a straight shooter, an honest cop who believes in what he's doing," Rizzo said. "I respect that a great deal. I also don't like Jimmy's name being smeared and his family being embarrassed in public. If there is anything I can do to help you, have Frank give me a call."

"I will," I said. "And thanks for the coffee."

* * *

"I would advise not to call upon Tony Rizzo for any reason, Jack," Kagan said as he drove us to the beach. "Any favor asked has to be repaid in kind, and you don't want to owe anything, not to Rizzo."

"I realize that," I said. "I just wanted to look into his eyes when I asked him about DeMarko."

"And what did you see?" Kagan said.

"If there was any doubt about Walt's innocence, it's been

removed," I said.

"And you can tell that from looking into his eyes?" Kagan said.

"Windows to the soul," I said.

"I thought mobsters didn't have souls," Kagan said.

"Nobody is born a mobster, or born bad, for that matter," I said. "Rizzo has a soul just like the rest of us. It's buried deep behind the eyes."

"And you can see it?" Kagan said.

"If you know what to look for," I said.

* * *

"These reports on Smith's street contacts are the funniest thing I've read in decades," Carly said when Kagan and I joined them at the table.

"Is there any truth to them?" Kagan said.

"Smith's initial contact with the FBI was a phone call where he reported he heard on the street that a disgruntled ex-employee of Jimmy DeMarko wanted to get even for being fired and had information concerning meetings between DeMarko and Walt. He reported to Smith that in his capacity as DeMarko's driver, he drove DeMarko to several meetings between DeMarko and Walt."

"No dates, no times, no locations," Harry said.

"It's bullshit, all of it," Carly said. "And Judge Brooks knows it. That's why he's allowing us to cross these morons in court."

"Who wants some lunch?" I said.

* * *

We talked witness strategy as we shoveled in Chinese food. It wouldn't be too difficult to discredit Smith and company on the stand and put doubt in the minds of the grand jury.

Napier would be banking on the six hundred grand.

In his place, so would we.

And it was a good strategy to follow.

We had no way to counter the six hundred thousand found in the safe deposit box.

As he ate some spicy chicken, Kagan said, "Whoever concocted this scheme is nothing short of a genius."

I agreed.

The questions remained.

Who?

And why?

* * *

"You went to see Tony Rizzo? Are you fucking nuts?" Walt said. "Have you gone completely crazy?"

We were in my backyard at the patio table.

"Too bad we can't get him on the stand," I said. "He's a big fan of yours."

"Oh, for God's sake."

"I know we've been down this road before, but who did you piss off enough to do this?" I said.

"Besides you and all of Elizabeth's relatives?" Walt said.

"Help me, Walt," I said. "I need a lead to follow."

"What happened with those reports Jane printed for you?" Walt said.

I stared at Walt for a few moments.

"I gotta go," I said.

"Wait."

"I'll call you later," I said.

"About what?" Walt called after me as I rushed inside the house.

# Chapter Twenty-four

Ibuilt a large bonfire in the trashcan, made a pot of coffee, and brought out the battery-powered camping lantern.

Thanks to Walt, I remembered the last thirty reports Jane gave me that I had neglected to read.

I scoured them as if they were the Dead Sea Scrolls.

When I reached the nineteenth report in the folder, my ears started to ring.

Yann Michael Reed. Age listed as forty-seven. IQ of 177 and that was in high school. Graduated MIT, top of his class. Went to work for a computer firm in Seattle, designing software for the banking and finance industry.

By the time he was thirty, Reed's skills were in such high demand that he quit his job, moved home, and went into business for himself. A few years after hanging the shingle over his door, Reed was one of the most sought-after web and software designers in the banking, financial, and stock market circles.

He married his high school sweetheart, bought a nice big house, and had a couple of kids. And thanks to his skills, Reed traveled to far and exotic places.

He designed hack-proof software for the banking, financial, and corporate world in a dozen countries. Often he was hired by major companies, including governments, to try and hack their systems. If he could—which was the case most of the time—hack a system, they would pay him handsomely to redesign it and make the system hack-proof.

Hack-proof to all but himself, that is. Early on, he realized that companies would never miss fractions of a penny in the profits. A quarter penny here, three quarters of a penny there, when spread out across billions and billions of dollars added up to many millions siphoned off to an account created by Reed that was hack-proof to anybody but himself.

After a few years of skimming, Reed had a fortune in ill-gotten gain.

The joke he must have found funny was the gain came from the very companies that hired him to protect them from hackers.

Like himself.

Reed's downfall came in the form of, what else, a woman.

On a trip to New York, Reed met a Russian woman who would become his mistress. He set her up in an apartment on Central Park West and paid her twenty thousand a month to be at his beck and call.

His wife first grew suspicious of Reed's affair when his trips to New York became more frequent, and he was never at the hotel he claimed to be staying at. She hired a private detective to follow Reed, and he reported back to her of the affair.

Enraged and not without knowledge of her husband's business practices, Reed's wife went to the police and asked to see a detective.

She hit the jackpot in then–Lieutenant Walt Grimes. She told Walt that her husband was a crook, stealing money from his clients using some kind of computer program.

After an initial investigation, Walt knew he was onto something big, but he also knew he needed help.

Walt recruited the FBI and after a six-month-long investigation, they gathered enough evidence against Reed for an indictment.

Walt and the FBI made a joint arrest. Walt testified in court, and Reed went away for seven years to Coleman prison in Florida.

Reed's wife filed for divorce and got most of his legitimate holdings and finances. She remarried and moved away about five years ago.

I grabbed Smith's file. Lo and behold, they both were in Coleman at the same time.

"They know each other," I said aloud.

Since his release from Coleman, Reed had returned home. He served every day of his seven-year sentence, so he wasn't obligated to meet with a parole officer.

As part of his sentence, Reed was forbidden to own a computer or work in the industry.

I set the file aside and called Jane's cell phone.

"Where are you?" I said.

"About to leave the office."

"Don't," I said. "I'll be right over."

* * *

"Yann Michael Reed?" Jane said. "Who names their kid Yann?"

"Greeks," I said. "Irish father, Greek mother."

"So, why am I interested in this loser?" Jane asked.

"He's no loser," I said. "Read his file. He has an IQ of 177."

"So, he's a smart loser," Jane said.

"He just happened to be in Coleman at the same time as Smith," I said.

"Along with thirteen hundred others," Jane said.

"Who just happened to move back here after their release," I said.

Jane looked at me. "I admit, it's a coincidence," she said.

"Come on, Jane. Police work 101, there is no such thing as coincidence."

"Maybe not, but…"

"Read his file," I said. "And I'll buy you a late dinner."

Jane read the file.

"Okay, so he was really smart and did a lot of bad things with those smarts," she said. "Besides being in the same prison at the same time as Smith, how are these two connected?"

"People do a lot of talking in prison," I said.

"People do a lot of things in prison, Jack."

"Just listen a minute," I said.

"Sure. Over dinner."

* * *

As she carved into a steak, Jane said, "I'm all ears, Jack."

"What if Reed spent his time in Coleman planning revenge against Walt?" I said.

"Walt wasn't alone," Jane said. "The FBI arrested him as well."

"I know that," I said. "But if I'm right, he's taking down Walt, and making the FBI look really foolish in the process."

"Any evidence of this?"

"Not a shred."

"And you want to do…?"

"Get the evidence I need to go after this guy."

Jane ate another piece of her steak. "I'm going to regret asking, but how?"

"He's not on parole, so he doesn't have to report in," I said. "But he's been out a year, so he must have a driver's license with an address on it."

"And you want me to get it for you?" Jane said.

"What can it hurt to check him out?" I said.

"With you involved, a lot," Jane said. "But I'll get it for you."

"Want dessert?" I said.

"Who doesn't?"

* * *

By the time we returned to Jane's office, it was after midnight. Just a few deputies were on duty with a few cars on patrol.

Jane did a search of Yann Michael Reed and gave me the address listed on his driver's license.

"How far can you go back on his license history?" I said.

Jane hunted around in her computer and showed the first license issued to Reed when he was sixteen. The address was the same.

"He's living with his mom," I said.

"Alright, enough violating people's privacy rights," Jane said. "I have to be on duty at nine."

"Want to come back to my place?" I said.

"I'll won't get any sleep, and I'll walk in here with bags under my eyes," Jane said. "Let's go."

# Chapter Twenty-five

Jane called her office and told her deputy taking calls that she needed to check something out and wouldn't be in until ten.

What she needed to check out was a few extra hours of sleep. She always kept a clean uniform in her cruiser and a small overnight bag.

When she emerged from the trailer looking fresh and crisp, she sat beside me with a large mug of coffee.

"I'm tired, Jack," she said. "When this term is up I've decided not to run for re-election."

"You said that two election cycles ago," I said.

"Twenty-four years is enough," Jane said. "How are we ever going to plan anything as a couple with me wearing the uniform?"

"When is your term up?"

"Two years."

"Let's talk about it after Walt is acquitted," I said.

"Someone's coming," Jane said.

"That would be Carly and her little rascals," I said.

Jane stood up. "Thanks for the coffee and nookie," she said. "Call me later."

I watched Jane's cruiser leave and Carly's limo arrive and didn't have to move a muscle.

Carly poked her head out of the limo. "Had breakfast yet?" she said.

* * *

We went to the diner and ordered breakfast specials.

Kagan planned to rehearse Walt one more time before the grand jury convened.

Carly and Harry planned a review of all paperwork in case they overlooked a detail or two.

"Napier is going to be tough to beat at the grand jury and even tougher in court if he gets an indictment," Carly said. "So we need to be sure of every question, of every answer, of every fucking detail, no matter how small or large."

"This is personal for you," Kagan said.

"That son of a bitch Napier nearly sent me to prison and ruined my life," Carly said. "I'd love nothing better than to shove the point of my stiletto heel up his bony ass."

"Let's not lose sight of the fact that it's Captain Grimes on trial for his life," Kagan said. "Not your stiletto heels."

"What about you, Bekker, what do you plan to do today?" Carly said.

"Take a ride in the country," I said.

* * *

The Reed home was a small house about forty-five minutes north of town. It was in the middle of a quiet, tree-lined street in a nice neighborhood.

A ten-year-old Ford sedan was parked in the driveway in front of a closed garage door. I parked across the street and watched the house for a while.

The curtains were drawn in all the visible windows. I couldn't tell if anybody was home. I decided to sit for a spell.

A year ago, I would have smoked three or four cigarettes while I waited.

Instead, I opened the lid on the deli container of coffee and took a sip.

By the time the deli container was empty, I was rewarded when the front door opened and Reed and his mother appeared. They walked to the car and got in. Reed drove.

I gave them a block lead and followed.

Reed took me to the highway for several exits, and then got off and drove to the mall. He parked outside the food court and held his mother by the arm as they walked to the entrance.

I parked a few rows back and took my time entering the food court. Mom was at a table. Reed was at the pizza stand. I wasn't hungry, but I went to the burger stand and got a burger and coffee.

I sat behind Reed and ate my burger. As he brought the pizza to his table, I used my cell phone to take a few photos of him.

As soon as my burger was consumed, I took my coffee and left the food court.

* * *

Kagan had come and gone by the time I reached my house.

I met with Walt in the backyard over a couple of glasses of cold lemonade.

"Tell me about Yann Michael Reed," I said.

"That's nine years ago, at least," Walt said.

"I know. I read the arrest report," I said. "Tell me about him."

"He was some kind of computer genius," Walt said. "Embezzled millions from his clients. It was his wife who fingered him after she found out he had a Russian mistress stashed in New York. I had to get the FBI involved, and we still couldn't crack that egg. It took a federal warrant for the FBI to confiscate all of his computer crap. I was acting lieutenant at the time. That case made it permanent. Now, mind telling me why the interest?"

"Reed and Smith were at Coleman at the same time," I said.

Walt looked at me. I could see the gears moving behind his eyes. "So they crossed paths," he said. "You don't think…?"

"How was Reed at the trial?" I said.

"As far as I remember, he never made a sound," Walt said. "Even when the judge pronounced sentence, he didn't say a thing."

"Did he take the stand in his own defense?" I said.

"No, but he did take the stand for the prosecutor," Walt said. "He spent more time staring at me than answering questions. I think back now, I remember he had those crazy Charles Manson eyes."

"He ever threaten you, say anything in court?"

"No, never. Even when we arrested him, he kept his mouth shut."

"Did you attend his sentencing hearing?"

Walt nodded. "The judge gave him the opportunity to speak, but he never said a word," Walt said. "Sentence was pronounced, and he was ushered off to prison."

"Did they recover all the stolen money?" I said.

"Hell if I know," Walt said. "They recovered a lot and paid what they could to the victims, but who really knows?"

"He's been out close to a year," I said. "Lives with his mother."

Walt looked at me. "Is it possible he teamed up with Smith to frame me?" he said.

"Anything is possible," I said.

"It could be a coincidence that they were at Coleman together, and nothing more."

"I don't believe in coincidence," I said. "I think he still has access to a lot of the money he embezzled, met Smith in Coleman, and concocted a scheme to get even with you and make the FBI look like fools in the process."

"Can you prove any of that?"

"No, not yet."

"I'm running out of time, Jack," Walt said. "No matter how many times Kagan rehearses me, and Carly discredits the witnesses in court, the six hundred thousand is a noose around my neck."

"I better get busy then," I said. "Before that noose tightens."

* * *

I parked across the street from the Reed home a few houses down and waited. The Ford sedan arrived near sunset, and I was ready with a digital camera that had a decent zoom lens.

Reed parked in the driveway, and between him and his mother, they carried a dozen shopping bags into the house.

While Reed carried bags, I got busy with the camera.

Once they were in for the night, I took off.

* * *

At the trailer, I powered up the computer and downloaded the photos I took of Reed.

I made some coffee and then drank a cup at the kitchen table while I reviewed the photos.

Reed was about six-foot-two, the same height as Walt. He was a bit thinner, had lighter hair, and had blue eyes to Walt's brown.

But, it was *possible*.

I used the landline phone to call Venus at home.

"Well, well, John Bekker," Venus said. "Let me guess, you need a favor."

"I do," I said.

"Concerning?"

"Walt, what else?"

"Knowing you, it could be anything," Venus said.

"Can you help?"

"I don't know, you haven't asked me anything yet."

"Face recognition that you use to help victims identify a suspect, can you construct something for me?" I said.

"When?"

"Tomorrow, say, around ten," I said. "I'll be bringing the Little Rascals."

"Who?"

"Walt's defense team."

Venus sighed heavily. "Only for Walt," she said. "Not for your dumb white ass."

"I owe you," I said.

"My house needs painting," Venus said.

# Chapter Twenty-six

Before anybody could hop out of the limo, I opened the front passenger door and got in beside the driver.

"We're taking a detour," I said.

From behind me, Carly asked, "Where?"

"Pat's Donuts," I said.

* * *

I sprung for three dozen donuts and a large box of joe. Two dozen went to the squad room, while a dozen went to Venus.

As she bit into a Boston cream donut, Venus said, "Grey."

"What's grey?" I said.

"The new color of my house," Venus said.

Kagan sipped coffee to wash down a bite of a chocolate donut and then said, "Maybe you should tell us what's going on here."

I handed Venus my camera. "Download the last dozen photos," I said. Then I withdrew the report on Reed from my jacket pocket and handed it to Kagan.

As Venus downloaded, Kagan, Carly and Harry read.

"I remember this case," Carly said. "I was a junior ADA at the time."

"He got out a year ago," I said. "He was also in Coleman with Smith."

"Photos are ready," Venus said.

I scanned the dozen photos and selected a decent front shot. "That one," I told Venus. "Let's use that one."

Venus swirled her chair around to face another computer. She pulled up her program and downloaded the photo I selected.

We ate donuts while she brought up the photo.

"Okay, close in on his face," I said.

Venus zoomed in a bit on Reed's face.

"Add twenty-five pounds so his face is puffier," I said.

We watched as Venus added flesh to Reed's face, making it softer and rounder.

"Darken his hair and style it like Walt's," I said.

Venus made the change to the hair.

"Now give him brown eyes like Walt's," I said.

Venus changed the eye color.

"What do you think?" I said.

Venus looked at me. Then she split the screen in half and pulled up a photo of Walt, so that he and Reed were side by side.

"If you saw Reed looking like this just once seven months ago and then were shown this photo of Walt, what would you think?" I said.

"I think you might think it's the same guy," Carly said.

"I think you might be right," I said. "Venus, can we get some hard copies of each and a side-by-side?"

"Sure, and don't forget grey is my favorite color," Venus said.

* * *

As the limo whisked us to my house, Kagan said, "What was all that 'my house, color grey' stuff back there?"

"I think in exchange for her services, I'm supposed to paint Venus's house," I said.

Carly thought that funny and cracked up laughing. "Bekker, you're such a sucker," she said. "All she really wants is a roll in the hay."

"Remember the earrings," I said.

"Earrings might take offense to you painting another woman's crotch," Carly said. "I mean, house."

"What in God's name are you people talking about?" Kagan said.

"You know, if I was that banker and I was shown the photo of Walt seven months after the fact, I might make the same identification he did," Harry said.

"I think that's Bekker's point," Carly said.

"I realize that, but are we going to use it in court?" Harry said.

"Do you know what an October surprise is?" Carly said.

"Right before an election, something bad is reported to hurt the candidate's chances," Harry said.

"Reed is going to be our October surprise," Carly said.

* * *

Walt looked at the photo comparison and shook his head. "Son of a bitch," he said.

"All it took was for Reed to darken his hair and eyes and get a little fat to pull it off," Carly said.

"I'm not…" Walt said.

"Especially after seven months," Harry said.

"We'll have the jury so confused, they'll have no choice but to dismiss," Kagan said.

"And what about this Reed?" Walt said. "Do you think if this is true, he's just going to sit on his hands while I walk?"

"No, I don't," I said. "Right now, the goal is to get you off. I'll work on Reed."

"Chin up, Walt," Carly said. "This is almost over. Alright, let's go. We have a new line of questioning to consider."

"Give me a minute," I said.

After Walt and I were alone, Walt looked at me. "Jack, I don't know what to say."

"How are you at painting houses?" I said.

* * *

While Carly, Kagan and Harry worked at the table, Regan, Oz and I hung out down at the beach.

Regan brought her little pug, Cuddles, and they splashed around a bit in the low tide waves.

"Look like Walt gonna be set free," Oz said.

"You never know what a grand jury is going to do, but it's looking better for Walt," I said.

"Hey, Dad, let's do a cookout!" Regan said.

"Sounds good," I said.

I stood and walked to the trailer. "Who's up for a cookout?" I said.

"Why not?" Carly said. "We plan to work until dark anyway."

"Call Campbell, tell her to bring the baby," I said.

I grabbed Oz and we drove to town. On the way, I called Jane and asked her to stop by.

At the market, I picked up steak tips, burgers, dogs, chicken, baked beans, rolls, and bags of chips.

Later, as the sun went down, I fired up the grill.

Campbell arrived with Settina and Regan took over.

A bit after that, Jane showed up in her cruiser.

"What are we celebrating?" Jane asked.

"Bekker is a lot smarter than he looks," Carly said.

"Well, hell, I thought everybody knew that," Jane said.

I grilled, Regan took care of Settina, and we ate in front of a large bonfire in the trashcan.

The sun went down and the bonfire burned low.

The limo whisked Regan and Oz home, so by nine o'clock, Jane and I were alone on the beach.

She smoked a cigarette as we both sipped from mugs of coffee.

"So, this little magic trick you pulled out of your hat might do the trick," Jane said.

She passed me the cigarette and I took a hit.

"You never know about a grand jury," I said. "A lot depends upon the presentation. Who does cross and how well it's received. But the odds are looking much better."

"And Venus put this together for you?" Jane said.

I gave her back the cigarette.

"For Walt," I said.

"Uh-huh. And what's the payment?" Jane said.

"What makes you think there's a payment?" I said.

Jane blew a smoke ring and flared her nostrils at me. "A: she's a woman. B: she has an itch. C: she wants you to scratch it," she said.

I looked at Jane.

"Choose your words carefully," she said.

"You're wearing the diamond earrings, not her, so I guess she'll just have to find another back scratcher," I said.

Jane shrugged. "Not bad. Not exactly Hemmingway, but not bad," she said. "Let's go for a romp."

"In the water?" I said.

Jane stood up and waked to the door of the trailer. "Sure," she said. "Afterwards."

# Chapter Twenty-seven

Walt's grand jury hearing began on Monday. Today was Saturday, and so far I've spent the morning parked diagonally across the street from the Reed home.

I showed up shortly before eight with two containers of coffee and an egg sandwich in a paper bag.

The Ford sedan was parked in the driveway.

The garage door was closed. I wondered why the Ford was in the driveway and not the garage.

Around ten o'clock, I got the answer when Reed emerged from the house wearing crisp jeans, a grey T-shirt, and white Nike sneakers. He backed the Ford out of the driveway, then returned to the garage and opened it to reveal a silver BMW 750i. He drove it to the curb, then returned the Ford to the driveway and closed the garage.

The BMW was at least eight or nine years old, but looked showroom new, probably because it didn't get much use while Reed was in prison.

Once he was behind the wheel of the BMW, Reed drove to the end of the block and turned left.

I followed, but gave him plenty of room.

It's hard not to spot a silver 750i on the road, even a used one. Reed had eight cylinders and nearly five hundred horsepower under the hood and could have smoked just about anything on the road, but he was in no hurry.

The slow speed chase took me to the highway, where Reed barely cracked sixty miles per hour.

I stayed six car lengths behind him for the fifteen-minute ride it took for him to exit onto a road that took us deeper into the suburbs.

After a few twists and turns, Reed pulled into the driveway of a small home on a tree-lined street and parked next to a Jeep Cherokee. I stayed on the corner while Reed went to the door, where he was greeted by a dark-haired woman.

Once Reed was inside, I turned and drove past the house and made note of the address that was displayed on the mailbox mounted on a wooden stake, and the license plate on the Jeep.

I couldn't risk being seen, so I drove to the end of the block and completely around it to the corner again, and parked where I could safely watch the house from a distance.

After thirty minutes of nothing, I drove home to the trailer.

* * *

Carly, Kagan and Harry were out front at the table when I arrived.

"Last minute tweaking before Monday," Carly said.

"Is Walt ready?" I said.

"He's been rehearsed as best as possible," Kagan said. "If he keeps his cool, he'll do alright."

I grabbed the chair next to Carly. "Who is doing which?" I said.

"I'm doing Smith and Phelps and Underwood," Carly said. "Frank will handle Walt, since he's rehearsed him."

"And the banker?" I said.

"Frank is more suited for that one," Carly said.

I went inside and made a pot of coffee. When it was ready, I brought it and four cups to the table and poured.

"What are our chances?" I said as I took a seat.

"Fair," Carly said.

"There is just no way to figure how a grand jury will vote," Kagan said.

I sipped my coffee and called Jane on my cell phone. "Are you working today?"

"Three to eleven," Jane said. "Covering for my senior deputy."

"Can I stop by for a bit?" I said.

I could hear Jane inhale on a cigarette. "What you're really asking is can I do you another favor?" she said.

"It's a small one," I said.

"Then, I'll settle for a small dinner," Jane said. "Around six."

"Small?" I said.

"Don't be late," Jane said and hung up.

I went inside to change, and then worked the heavy bag for a bit, switched over to the speed bag, jumped rope, and did sets of elevated push-ups.

"We're knocking off for today," Carly said, when I took my chair to strap on the ankle weights. "We'll meet at the courthouse on Monday at ten o'clock for Walt's hearing."

As I strapped on an ankle weight, I nodded.

"We've done everything we can," Kagan said.

"I know," I said, as I strapped on the second ankle weight.

"Try to relax, Bekker," Carly said.

After they left, I went down to the beach for a run.

I jogged for thirty minutes before making a U-turn and heading back. With fifteen minutes left, I veered into ankle-deep water, and within seconds, my sneakers and ankle weights were weighted down with water.

The final five minutes had my lungs and legs burning.

I collapsed into my chair and removed the ankle weights, socks and sneakers.

My cell phone rang and I checked the incoming number.

"Hi sweetheart," I said.

"Are you coming home tonight?" Regan said.

"Later, after I'm done working on a few things," I said.

"Uncle Walt is acting strange," Regan said.

"What do you mean?"

"All nervous and stuff," Regan said.

"It's understandable," I said. "The hearing is on Monday. Try to keep him occupied. I'll be home around nine."

"Okay," Regan said. "Nine, and don't be late."

* * *

Jane ran the license plate from the Jeep Cherokee.

"Rosamund Riker," Jane said. "Middle name Rose. Age listed as thirty-four. Is the address on the license the same as you wrote down?"

"Yes."

"So, who is she?"

"I don't know," I said. "Possibly Reed's girlfriend and accomplice."

"Clean driving record except for a parking ticket when she was eighteen," Jane said.

"Check her arrest record," I said.

Jane sighed, but checked. "Clean," she said.

"Not if she's tied in with Reed she's not," I said. "Check the plate on the BMW."

Jane pulled up the information. "Nine years old and registered to Reed."

"He drove it from his mother's house to this Riker woman's place this morning," I said.

"Are you tailing this guy?"

"I did," I said. "But I know the stalker laws and it was from a safe distance."

"You have somewhat reasonable cause given the circumstances, and the fact that you're a licensed private investigator," Jane said.

"I know all that," I said. "I also know this Reed is behind all this."

Jane lit a cigarette. "I know you, Jack. You're not going to stop. At least, let me help so we keep it somewhat legal."

I agreed with a nod. "Let's grab a bite," I said. "I promised Regan I'd be home by nine."

* * *

Jane was in the mood for real Italian pizza. About a mile from her office is a pizza joint that advertises "The Best Pizza Outside Of The Bronx."

The owner was a seventy-nine-year-old man named Sal, and he opened the restaurant some forty years ago after relocating from the Bronx. His two sons worked the brick oven while Sal waited tables.

We ordered a large pie, garlic rolls, and two soft drinks.

"Other than surveillance, how can I find out who this Riker is and what she does?" I said.

"You have no cause for a warrant," Jane said. "Or a wiretap, or a background check on her employer."

"*If* she has an employer," I said. "Could you run a search on her employment history?"

"Tonight?"

"Walt's hearing is Monday," I said. "In a regular trial, he might have a shot at an acquittal based on the evidence, or at least a mistrial. But at a grand jury hearing, despite the evidence contrary to the prosecutor's case, they're going to want to know where the six hundred thousand came from. I've done the math. Walt loses."

Jane looked at me. "I'll call you later," she said.

"Take Sunday off," I said. "We'll make it a beach day with Regan and Oz."

Jane nodded. "Jack, you can only do what you can do," she said. "After that…"

* * *

After I dropped Jane off at her office, I drove straight to my house.

Oz, Regan and Elizabeth were in the living room.

"What's going on?" I said.

"I've never seen him like this," Elizabeth said.

"Where is he?" I said.

"Backyard," Oz said.

I went to the kitchen and opened the sliding glass doors and stepped out into the yard.

Walt was in a frenzy, circling the lawn and talking to himself.

"Walt?" I said.

He spun and looked at me. Even in near darkness, I could see the panic and fear in his eyes.

"Thirty plus years as a cop and I never took a nickel," he said. "Never skirted the law, never even fixed a fucking parking ticket, and for what?"

"Walt, calm down," I said.

"There going to stick me in a cell, Jack," Walt said. "For the rest of my life, and for something I didn't do. What happens to Elizabeth when I'm gone and they take away my pension? Who takes care of her Jack? Who?"

"Walt, this isn't doing any good," I said.

He grabbed a patio chair and flung it against the fence.

"Goddammit," Walt screamed.

I took a step toward Walt, and he grabbed another chair and flung it against the ground.

"Not one fucking nickel did I ever take," he screamed.

"I know that," I said.

He placed his hands under the table and upended it.

I rushed him and encircled his arms from behind.

"Let me go, you fucking ape," Walt said.

"Not until you calm down," I said.

Walt fought hard, flailing out with his legs, but I increased the pressure and he slowly weakened.

"I can't… breathe," Walt said.

I bent him forward and placed him on his knees, then shoved him to the grass and placed one foot on his back.

Gasping, Walt said, "Let me up."

"As soon as you calm down," I said.

"I'm calm, damn you. Now let me up."

"I don't think you're calm," I said.

"I'm fucking calm," Walt said. "You want it in writing?"

I removed my foot and retrieved the chairs and righted the table, then took a seat. Slowly, Walt stood up and took a chair opposite me.

"I have grass stains on my shirt," he said.

Elizabeth came out and hugged Walt.

"Come inside and I'll wash the shirt," she said.

Walt stood and they entered the house.
Regan came out and sat next to me.
"Jeez," she said.
I couldn't agree more.

# Chapter Twenty-eight

While Regan tossed a Frisbee to Jane, Oz patted Molly the cat, who was sleeping on his lap. Cuddle the pug tried in vain to snare the Frisbee, and I warmed up the grill.

"Twenty minutes to lunch," I announced.

Regan gave the Frisbee to Cuddles, and she and Jane ran to the water and dove in.

I tossed burgers, dogs and chicken onto the grill. "How is it coming with that developer?" I asked Oz.

"Man say construction start three months after we clear out," Oz said. "I told him we want a three bedroom facing the ocean on the first floor. I told him we put eighty thousand down. He say to come look at floor plans."

"Set it up, we'll go look," I said.

"I'll give him a call tomorrow," Oz said.

As I turned burgers and chicken, I looked down at the water, and Regan and Jane were engaged in conversation.

Beside me, Cuddles begged for scraps and I tossed him a small piece of chicken.

On the table, my cell phone rang. It was Carly.

"Bekker, I need a favor," she said.

"Who doesn't?" I said.

"I called your house and Walt said Regan was with you," Carly said. "Our nannies are off today, and Campbell has tickets to the road version of Hamilton. Do you think Regan can baby-sit?"

"Ask Regan," I said. "Hold on a moment."

Regan and Jane were walking toward the trailer, and I waved Regan over. "Phone," I said.

She took the phone, listened for a second and said, "Sure, I'd love to. What time?"

After she hung up, Regan said, "I have to be home by five, okay?"

"Oz, take my car," I said. "I won't need it until the morning. I'll get a ride from Jane."

We ate lunch, took a swim, and tossed the Frisbee around until four o'clock. Oz took my car and drove Regan back to the house.

Jane and I lazed around on lounge chairs and drank coffee.

I told her what happened yesterday with Walt.

"I'm not surprised the strain is getting to him," Jane said. "The man has been a cop his entire adult life. Patrolman, detective, sergeant, lieutenant and captain. And now that he's retiring, he faces the rest of his life in prison. Me, I'd go ballistic."

"He's more worried about Elizabeth than himself," I said.

"I can understand that, too," Jane said.

"Anything on Riker?" I said.

"If she works, it hasn't been recently," Jane said. "She was a hair dresser at one of those modern super-cut places until about nine months ago. Nothing since."

I sipped some coffee and allowed my thoughts to roam free. "The house in her name?" I said.

"She was married," Jane said. "Divorced about six years ago. She got the house and the mortgage."

"If she doesn't work, how does she pay it?" I said.

"Her checkbook has a few thousand in it," Jane said. "About seven thousand in savings. She should be broke, but that Cherokee she drives is new and goes for around forty thousand with all the options tacked on."

I sipped from my cup. "She'd be good with hair and makeup, wouldn't she?" I said.

Jane nodded. "She would."

"Reed found himself a girlfriend to help him plot his revenge," I said.

"Assuming, and it's a big assumption, that Reed has money stashed away someplace," Jane said.

"The police and FBI reports from nine years ago all state that there might be more money stashed away someplace," I said. "Just because they didn't find it, doesn't mean it doesn't exist."

"So… he finds a woman to help him with hair and makeup so he can pass for Walt?" Jane said.

"Two can travel more invisible than one," I said. "Say, on a vacation to Grand Cayman."

Jane looked at me. "A couple enjoying the sun and fun is less conspicuous than a man traveling alone," she said.

"Can you find out if she has a valid passport and recently took a trip to the Cayman Islands?" I said.

"That could take some time," Jane said.

"I know. Time we got," I said. "Walt is going to lose tomorrow, be indicted and that gives us time to work with, as much as three months, if the judge is reasonable."

"A lot can happen in three months," Jane said.

"A great deal," I said.

Jane took my hand. "Let's go inside and have us a swim," she said. "You know, to relieve some stress."

* * *

Jane and I sat in her cruiser for a few minutes before I went back inside.

"The transport van will be by at eight o'clock to pick up Walt and take him to court," Jane said. "Am I going to need more than two deputies?"

"I'll make sure it's okay," I said.

"This is the last thing I ever expected to do," Jane said.

We parted with a kiss, and I entered the house to find Oz, Walt and Elizabeth watching a movie on Netflix.

"Regan called and said she'll be home around midnight," Elizabeth said.

I nodded, went to the kitchen, grabbed a can of ginger ale from the fridge, and sat in the backyard at the patio table.

A few minutes later, Walt came out and joined me.

"I'm ready for tomorrow," he said. "I've tossed it around in my head looking for an answer, and I know I'm going to be indicted. As good as Carly and Kagan are, there is no explanation for the money."

I sipped some ginger ale and set the can on the table. "Three months, if the judge is reasonable," I said. "An indictment buys us three months. A lot can happen in three months."

Walt picked up the can of ginger ale and took a sip. "I wish I didn't quit smoking," he said.

"Me, too," I said.

"What time will they be by to pick me up?"

"Eight o'clock."

"I wish you didn't quit drinking," Walt said.

"Me, too."

"Come on, let's make some popcorn and watch the rest of the movie," Walt said.

# Chapter Twenty-nine

We ate breakfast at seven and then Walt dressed for court. He wore a blue pin-striped suit, white shirt, red tie, and black shoes.

At eight o'clock, Oz, Regan, Elizabeth and I gathered in front of my house to await the sheriff's transport van.

The van arrived right on time and I walked with Walt to the curb.

Two deputies got out and one deputy had the cuffs ready.

"Sorry about this, Captain Grimes," the deputy said.

Walt looked at the cuffs and extended his wrists. "It's your job," Walt said. "Do it."

The deputy snapped on the cuffs and Walt got into the rear of the van. He looked back at me. "See you in court," Walt said.

I watched the van take Walt away, and then I walked back to the house where Elizabeth and Regan were in tears.

"Liz, we have to leave in thirty minutes," I said.

"I'll be ready," Elizabeth said.

* * *

The opening act for the grand jury was FBI Agent Thomas Underwood.

Napier got things rolling.

I sat with Elizabeth behind the defense table. Walt sat at the table with Carly, Kagan and Harry.

Brooks kept his word and closed the courtroom to the public and the media.

Under Napier's guidance, Underwood painted a picture of the timeline leading up to Walt's arrest. From Smith's involvement with the Internal Affairs Division to Phelps taking it to the FBI, and then the constant monitoring of Walt, to Smith's street information concerning the bank in Grand Cayman. Under cross, Underwood explained how the investigation took six months, culminating with the six hundred thousand dollars found in the Cayman bank and Walt's arrest at his home.

Napier had Underwood on the stand for two hours.

After Brooks called for a thirty-minute break, Underwood was back on the stand crossed by Carly.

She brilliantly blew holes in Underwood's timeline. Smith's information came off like Swiss cheese, and how convenient for everyone involved that Jimmy DeMarko just happened to die in the middle of it all.

Underwood nearly lost his composure, but he gained points when his final statement was that Smith's information led them to the six hundred thousand dollars in a safe deposit box registered to Captain Walter Grimes.

Brooks ended the day and Walt was smuggled out the back door to the waiting transport van.

Napier and company took questions on the courthouse steps.

We skirted past the freak show to the limo and took off for home.

* * *

We had dinner in the backyard at the patio table.

"If I had to give us a grade today, it's a C plus," Carly said.

"I have to go with a B minus," Kagan said. "You tore enough holes in Underwood's testimony to cast a slight doubt in the grand jury's minds."

"Any fool can see Walt is innocent," Elizabeth said. "All that nonsense about informants and dead mobsters, it's like a second rate mystery novel."

"What's up for tomorrow?" Walt said.

"Phelps," Carly said. "And then Smith."

"That ought to be fun," Walt said.

After dinner, I called Jane.

* * *

Jane got out of her cruiser wearing jeans, sneakers, and a yellow sweatshirt. A file was tucked under her left arm. Her service weapon was on her right hip. I had a fire going in the trashcan, and she glowed in the light as she walked toward me.

I stood up from my chair and greeted Jane with a kiss and a mug of fresh coffee.

"How did it go?" Jane said as she took the chair next to mine.

"C minus or B plus, according to Carly and Kagan," I said.

"And according to you?" Jane said.

"We lost," I said. "Carly poked enough holes in Underwood's testimony to sink the Titanic, but the unanswered question left hanging in the air is where did the six hundred thousand come from?"

"Tomorrow?"

"Phelps takes the stand and possibly Smith, if there is time," I said. "What's in the file?"

Jane handed me the file. "Rosamund Rose isn't such a good girl after all," she said.

I opened the file. It was a sealed juvenile record.

"Nothing as an adult?" I said.

"No, but once a bad girl, always a bad girl," Jane said.

"What would it take to unseal her record?"

"A court order from a judge," Jane said. "For which we have no credible reason to ask."

"It doesn't matter," I said. "Like you said, once a bad girl, always a bad girl, and now we know she isn't Snow White, and my theory about Reed just got stronger."

"You're going to need more than a theory to keep Walt from prison," Jane said. "You're going to need a damn miracle."

* * *

Napier needed only one hour with Phelps on the stand. Napier's questions centered around Smith contacting Phelps with information he obtained on the street concerning a police captain involved in illegal activity with Jimmy DeMarko.

Phelps outlined his investigation into Walt's activities and told how he felt it warranted the attention of the FBI, since Jimmy DeMarko was a known mobster and racketeer.

When Phelps was done, Carly took over and shredded Phelps's timeline and Smith's credibility as a confidential informant based on written reports by Phelps and also by Underwood.

Brooks ordered a ninety-minute break for lunch, and court resumed at two o'clock.

Napier took about an hour to question Smith on his involvement as a confidential informant.

Smith had obviously been well-coached and handled himself well, politely answering Napier's questions without straying or volunteering information. Napier and Smith painted a timeline of events for the grand jury that covered Smith's release from prison to his hearing bits of information on the street to Smith contacting the Internal Affairs Division.

After Napier retired, Carly went after Smith like a pit-bull on a bone. She peppered him with non-stop questions that tied him up and confused him. After an hour, Carly tore Smith's timeline to ribbons, and as I watched Napier, I could see in his eyes that he lost that round.

* * *

"Today was a draw," Kagan said. "We exchanged queens."

"Down zero to one won't get us a dismissal," Carly said. "Bekker, anymore coffee?"

I got up from my chair, went inside the trailer, and returned with a fresh pot. After filling four mugs, I took my chair.

"Walt is as ready as he'll ever be for the stand," Kagan said. "As long as he holds his mud, he'll do fine."

"Napier wants this to go to trial," Carly said. "The gloves will come off tomorrow."

"This isn't my first rodeo," Kagan said. "And Napier is overconfident."

"Let's hope there is time for Cena to take the stand tomorrow," Carly said.

I sipped some coffee and looked at Kagan. "Why not let Harry cross Cena?" I said.

"What?" Kagan said.

"Did you say…?" Carly said.

"Me?" Harry said.

"This is no time for jokes, Bekker," Carly said.

"I'm not joking," I said. "No offense, Harry, but look at the guy. He's the last person in the world you'd expect to handle cross on Cena. Plus, they'll never see him coming."

Kagan and Carly exchanged looks.

"What do you think, Harry?" Kagan said.

"Like Mr. Bekker said, they'll never see me coming," Harry said.

"We have work to do," Carly said. "Bekker, better order some food."

# Chapter Thirty

Napier tore into Walt without mercy.

For ninety minutes, Napier fired questions at Walt, and to Walt's credit, he wasn't rattled or thrown off his game.

In the end, Walt had no answer to the question of where the money came from. I could see in the eyes of the grand jury, they wondered the same thing.

After a thirty-minute recess, Walt was back on the stand being crossed by Kagan.

Kagan was masterful and his line of questioning was brilliant. I watched the seeds of doubt in the eyes of the grand jury take root, as Kagan drove home the point that no matter hard the FBI tried, they couldn't prove that Walt traveled to Grand Cayman.

Brooks called for a ninety-minute recess for lunch and requested we wrap it up by going late with Cena.

* * *

We ate at a diner across the street from the courthouse.

"You're up, Harry," Kagan said. "I'd call today a draw, and that's all we need from you is another draw to give the grand jury a reason to return a dismissal."

"I'll do my best," Harry said.

"Don't be nervous, Harry," Carly said. "The grand jury will see that and react to it, and not in a good way."

"I know," Harry said.

"Napier will open with Cena," Kagan said. "Pay attention to Cena's body language and tone. Pick up on any little chip in his armor and use that in your questioning. Save the photo lineup for last. Let him get nice and comfortable, and then go for the throat."

Carly nodded. "The *throat*," she said.

* * *

When court resumed, Napier called Cena to the stand. His questions centered around Cena being able to identify Walt as the man who opened the safe deposit account at his bank on Grand Cayman.

Cena, when asked to identify Walt, pointed to him at the defense table.

Napier then asked Cena to identify the card with Walt's handwriting on it, and Cena said it was the card from his bank that Walt filled out the day he opened the account.

Napier rested and Harry stood up and approached the witness stand.

"Mr. Cena, how are you?" Harry said.

"Fine," Cena said.

Harry picked up a file from the evidence table. "Now, a few moments ago, you identified the signature card from your bank as the one filled out by Mr. Grimes. Is that correct?"

"Yes," Cena said.

"That's funny, because this report from the William Tavers Detective Agency, where Mr. Tavers is a well known handwriting specialist, declares the handwriting on the card to be a fraud," Harry said. He handed the report to the jury foreman. "How do you explain that, Mr. Cena?"

"I can't," Cena said. "I can only tell you what I witnessed."

"And what did you witness, Mr. Cena?" Harry said.

"Mr. Grimes signing a signature card in my bank," Cena said.

Harry pointed to Walt. "Is that Mr. Grimes seated at the defense table?"

"Yes," Cena said.

"The same man you identified in a photo lineup not once but twice?" Harry said.

Napier jumped to his feet. "Your honor, the People object to this line of questioning," he said.

"On what grounds?" Brooks said.

"We've covered the photo lineup a dozen times already," Napier said.

"So, one more time won't hurt," Brooks said.

"Your honor…" Napier said.

"Sit down, Mr. Napier," Brooks cautioned.

Napier sat.

"Now Mr. Cena, could you please identify Mr. Grimes from the photo lineup you identified him from just a few weeks ago?" Harry asked, and picked up a file from the evidence table.

"Take your time, Mr. Cena," Harry said, as he handed the file to him.

Cena looked at the photo lineup. "Number four," he said.

"Are you sure?" Harry said.

"I'm positive," Cena said. "Number four."

Harry took the file. "Your honor, the man Mr. Cena identified as Captain Walter Grimes is a photo of someone who looks like Captain Grimes, but is, in fact, not," he said.

Napier lost his mind objecting, as Harry showed the lineup card to Brooks.

Napier objected a half dozen times, but the damage was already done.

The day ended on a high note.

"We'll hear closing arguments tomorrow at ten o'clock," Brooks said.

* * *

"Carly has the most experience at closing arguments," Kagan said.

We were at the trailer where Carly was making notes on a legal pad.

"Should I order some dinner?" I said.

Carly looked up at me. "Meat. Red meat," she said. "And a lot of it."

"I'll go to town and hit the grocery store," I said.

An hour later, I was grilling steak tips, burgers, dogs, and baked potatoes.

Carly rehearsed her closing argument while we ate.

It was good, bordering on great, but was it enough to avoid an indictment?

By nine o'clock, the limo took the gang of three home, and I drove to my house.

Walt was taking in the cooler night air in the backyard while Regan, Elizabeth and Oz watched a movie.

I grabbed two cans of ginger ale from the fridge and joined Walt.

"What do you think my chances are tomorrow?" Walt said.

"Fair," I said.

"That photo thing, Napier didn't know about it?" Walt said.

"No."

Walt sipped some ginger ale.

So did I.

"I know Carly and Kagan are working pro bono, and Harry is paid by the city, but you're picking up the tab for everything else," Walt said. "It must be costing you a pretty penny."

"For better or worse, right?" I said.

# Chapter Thirty-one

Napier's closing argument lasted less than ten minutes. He instructed the grand jury to disregard the parlor tricks provided by the defense and concentrate on one vital piece of evidence.

"The one fact they can't explain away is the six hundred thousand dollars found in the safe deposit box issued to the defendant," Napier said. "There is no magic trick or sleight of hand to refute that one simple fact. You must indict if only to get to the bottom of where this money came from and how it wound up in the hands of Police Captain Walter Grimes?"

Carly spoke for about twenty minutes. She was brilliant and covered all the holes in Napier's prosecution with pinpoint accuracy.

"There is too much at stake here to ignore the discrepancies in the People's case against Captain Grimes," she said. "The sketchy confidential informants, the handwriting expert who wrote a sworn statement to the court that the signature on the bank card is fraudulent, the misidentification in the photo lineup, these are all facts that you can't ignore. You must weigh the People's case against these facts and reach the conclusion that Captain Grimes is the victim of a plot against him, and the only way to uncover that plot is through a dismissal of the charges against Captain Grimes, and by launching an investigation into the people who plotted against him."

The jury deliberated for nearly four hours.

We waited in the hallway and the courthouse cafeteria. Walt waited in the holding cell in the basement.

Finally, a court officer called us back into the courtroom.

The jury foreman spoke. "Your honor, we have weighed all the evidence on both sides, and we feel we must indict in order for the People to get to the bottom of the six hundred thousand dollars found in the bank on Grand Cayman," he said.

Brooks dismissed the jury.

"Trial in the case of the People v. Captain Walter Grimes is set for three months from today," Brooks said.

"Your honor, the defense requests that Captain Grimes be allowed to continue house arrest while we prepare for trial," Carly said.

"Granted," Brooks said.

* * *

"Son of a bitch, this makes me mad," Kagan said. "That grand jury knows damn fucking well Grimes is innocent. Even Napier knows it at this point."

"Calm down, Frank," Carly said. "You having a stroke won't help anything."

We were in the limo, riding back to the beach.

Harry sighed openly. "I'll probably be reassigned," he said.

Kagan looked across the back seats at me. "I'll make a few calls and…"

"No, Frank, Walt wouldn't want that," I said.

"Ask Walt if he wants to rot in a cell until he's eighty-five years old," Hagan said.

"I'm staying on," Carly said. "That fucking Napier."

Kagan looked at Carly. "If you want me, I'll stay on, too," he said.

Carly looked at Harry. "Let's keep the band together, Harry," she said.

"I'll request it," Harry said.

"A trial changes everything," Carly said. "We'll need a real office with law books and a conference table."

Kagan inhaled and sighed softly. "Fine, we can use mine," he said.

When we reached the trailer, I made a pot of coffee, and we sat in chairs and watched the ocean for a while.

"I guess we'll pack up and meet at Frank's office in the morning," Carly said. "Bekker, we won't need this computer, so…"

"I'll give it to Regan," I said.

"Will you…?" Carly said.

"Stay on?" I said. "If you need me to."

* * *

"Carly and Kagan have agreed to continue to represent you, and Harry is going to request to stay on as well," I said.

"And you?" Walt said.

"I'm one hundred percent behind you," I said.

We were at the patio table in the backyard. We had mugs of coffee and sipped and were silent for a few moments.

"I can't let you spend any more of your own money," Walt said.

"Your salary and pension is suspended, and what you have in the bank is for Liz," I said. "And besides, I tucked away some good paychecks on the Sample case and a few insurance fraud cases. Carly and Kagan are working pro bono, so stop talking garbage."

Walt sipped, sighed and said, "Three months to trial, I'm going to go stir crazy."

"I'll ask Carly to submit a request to the judge, see if we can get you some playground time," I said. "In the meantime, stay cool."

* * *

I parked on the corner where I had a good view of Reed's house and waited. The Ford was parked in the driveway. The garage door was closed.

I came armed with a roast beef sandwich, a can of ginger ale, and a thermos of coffee.

The sandwich and ginger ale went during the first hour. The sun went down and lights in the Reed home came on during the second.

I was working on the thermos when Reed appeared, moved the Ford, opened the garage and drove off in the 750i.

There wasn't any hurry. I knew where Reed was headed. I gave him a few minutes, started the car and drove to Rosamund Riker's home.

The drive took about twenty minutes.

As I drove past Riker's home, I saw that the 750i was parked next to her Cherokee again.

I turned around and drove home to the beach, made some coffee and a bonfire, and sat and did some thinking.

With an IQ north of one seventy, Reed was more than just a computer genius.

He was forbidden by law to own a computer as part of his sentencing.

That didn't mean he couldn't have a girlfriend who owned one.

What's that old saying, it takes one to know one?

In this case, to catch a genius, I needed a genius.

One just as crazy as Reed.

# Chapter Thirty-two

Shortly after sunrise, I was working on the heavy bag. I gave it about thirty minutes before switching over to the speed bag for another thirty, then did ten sets on the elevated push-up stand, and ended with a dozen sets of stomach crunches.

Workouts were my think tank. Thoughts flowed and ideas took shape while my body sweated and muscles burned.

After a shower, I put on a lightweight tan suit and drove my car to the Crist mansion.

"Bekker, that car of yours is an embarrassment," Campbell said when she opened the door to me.

"Nice to see you, too, Campbell," I said.

"If you're looking for Carly, she left for Kagan's office about twenty minutes ago," Campbell said.

"I'm actually here to see you," I said.

"Well, come into the kitchen then," Campbell said.

I followed her to the kitchen, a room about the size of my entire house.

"Sit," Campbell ordered.

I took a chair at the butcher block table for twelve. Campbell brought over two mugs of coffee from the espresso machine on her marble counter.

She sat next to me, lit a cigarette and said, "You need something. What do you need?"

"Can I use your jet one more time and can you not tell Carly about it?" I said.

"I don't keep secrets from her, Bekker," Campbell said. "It's not healthy in a relationship to keep secrets."

"It's not a secret if I tell her," I said.

"Where and when?"

"White Plains, New York, tomorrow morning," I said.

"What's in White Plains?" Campbell said.

"A genius," I said.

"Who can help Carly with the trial?"

"Yes."

She passed me the cigarette and I took a hit and passed it back.

"Do you know how much it costs to run that plane, even for a short flight?"

"I do," I said.

"And you can't just fly commercial because…?"

"Regan is still very uncomfortable on regular flights, and I need her to go with me," I said.

Campbell sighed softly. "Well, I haven't been shopping in Manhattan in a while," she said.

"Thank you," I said. "And I owe you one."

"Seems like more than one," Campbell said. "But who's keeping track?"

* * *

"Again with this rich doll and her private jet," Jane said when I told her I was going to White Plains.

"I need Regan to go with me, and she's still too anxious for regular flights," I said. "On a crowded plane, her anxiety acts up and I need her to be calm."

"So you turn to that pale drink of water and her jet?" Jane said.

"She's the only one I know who has one," I said.

Jane sat on the old lawn chair in front of the trailer and lit a cigarette. "How come you don't know any *ugly* rich women?" she said.

"Just lucky, I guess," I said.

"You are definitely asking for a black eye," Jane said.

"It's only one day," I said.

"Well, what's in White Plains?" Jane said.

"Help," I said. "Much needed help."

"For Walt?"

I nodded.

"So, why is the daughter of a dead mob boss so fond of Walt?" Jane said.

"She's not," I said. "But she *is* fond of Carly, and Carly wants to win, if only to get revenge against Napier. Either way, it helps Walt."

"And you'll repay this act of kindness *how*?" Jane said.

"Paint her house," I said.

Jane's eyes turned dark for a few seconds and I thought a black eye was forthcoming. Then her face softened and she flicked away the cigarette and stood up. "Come on," she said and took my hand. "The least you can do is paint *my* house."

* * *

I picked up Regan at eight o'clock the next morning. She tossed her overnight bag into the trunk of my car and then got into the passenger seat.

"Where are we going that's such a secret?" Regan said.

"It's not a secret," I said. "I just haven't told you yet."

"And?"

"White Plains," I said.

Regan looked at me. "Dad?"

"I know, but I really need your help with this," I said.

"You owe me one, Dad," Regan said. "A big one."

"Our house doesn't need painting," I said.

"What?"

* * *

Regan held Settina on her lap while Campbell and I ate egg sandwiches with coffee.

"An Uber cab will pick us up at the private airport in White Plains," I told Regan. "We shouldn't be more than a few hours."

"I don't want to sit in traffic, so meet me at the hotel in Manhattan," Campbell said.

Regan placed Settina over her right shoulder, and the baby closed her eyes.

A little while later we landed in White Plains, New York. The private airport was for corporate travelers that visited the half dozen major companies headquartered there.

Included in that group were ITT, Dannon, Krasdale Foods, Heineken, Nine West, and Sample Ice Tea.

Our destination was Sample Ice Tea.

A little more than a year ago, I was asked to baby-sit the sixth child of the founder of the Sample Ice Tea Company.

Wally Sample was the forty-year-old black sheep of the family, a degenerate gambler who owed money to all of Vegas, Atlantic City, and to a few loan sharks. Wally's father left a clause in his will that Wally could not become a partner in the company unless he could prove he could go thirty days without gambling in any form.

I was hired to make sure that Wally didn't gamble for those thirty days leading up to his birthday.

As it turned out, Wally wasn't gambling for the sake of gambling, but was a mathematical genius using gambling to formulate theories of mathematical probabilities. After a few twists and turns that involved company in-fighting, a murder attempt, a kidnapping, and an exploding house, Wally took his seat at the Sample table as a partner.

Shaped like a pear, barely five-foot-six inches tall, Wally wore glasses and dressed like a slob, but hidden in that unkempt head of his was an Einstein-sized brain.

After the cab dropped us off at the Sample Ice Tea building, Regan said, "We're going to see Wally, aren't we?"

"Yes," I said.

"That's why you wanted me along, to keep him calm?"

"Also yes."

"So you won't get upset when I ask for a favor?"

"I'll do my best," I said. "What's the favor?"

"I'll tell you later," Regan said.

We checked in at the security desk. After a phone call, a guard issued us visitors' passes, and we took the private elevator to the floor reserved for the Sample family.

We were greeted at the elevator by Robert Jr., the senior member of the Sample family and company president.

"Mr. Bekker, nice to see you again," he said as we shook hands.

"This is my daughter Regan," I said.

"Hello, Regan," Robert said.

"Hello, sir," Regan said.

"I need a favor," I said. "From Wally."

"I figured," Robert said. "I'll take you to Wally's office."

We followed Robert along the hallway to an office door made of glass with gold lettering etched into it.

*Wally Sample, Vice President* the etching read.

Robert knocked and opened the door.

"Wally, you have visitors," Robert said.

Regan and I stepped into the office. It was a large room filled with clutter. A desk beside a window was covered with stacks and stacks of papers. Two file cabinets were so stuffed the doors wouldn't close. A massive blackboard took up an entire wall. It was covered with mathematical equations.

Wally, in all his disheveled genius, was at the blackboard with a piece of chalk in his right hand.

"Wally, you have guests," Robert said.

Wally turned and looked at us. His entire round face seemed to burst into a wide smile.

"Mister Bekker, Regan, what are you doing here?" Wally said. "Am I in trouble again? Robert, why didn't you tell me Mr. Bekker was here? Mr. Bekker, let me show you what I'm working on. See, the probability of accidents on the road that slows delivery can be lessened if… would you care for some tea or coffee? I can send down for… wait, is it lunch time? Robert, is it time for lunch? I really need a watch. Robert, why don't I have a watch?"

Regan rolled her eyes. "Oh boy," she said.

"Wally, we need to talk," I said.

"It's lunch time, isn't it?" Wally said.

* * *

The Sample family had a private dining room with a chef on duty for breakfast, lunch, and dinner, need be.

We ordered BLTs with fries. The BLT was served with one-inch thick slices of whole wheat bread, slightly toasted. The tomato slices were fresh and crisp, as was the lettuce, and the bacon was maple flavored, thick cut. The fries were the thickest cut and crispiest I've ever tasted.

"This is the best sandwich I've ever had," Regan said.

"I'm a big fan of lettuce," Wally said. "Especially when it's nice and crisp with just the right amount of pepper and salt."

"Wally, I need your help," I said.

"I have trouble sometimes, too. Cut it in half and it's easier to bite," Wally said.

"Oh boy," Regan said.

"I'm not talking about the sandwich," I said.

"No?" Wally said.

"Do you remember Captain Grimes?" I said.

* * *

As we walked along the hallway, Wally said, "I need to check with Robert."

"Sure," I said.

We reached Robert's office and Wally tapped on the glass door, and when it opened, we stepped in.

"Robert, I need to go with Mr. Bekker for a few days," Wally said. "He needs my help."

Robert sprang up from behind his desk and rushed over to us.

"By all means, Wally, please, go help your friends," Robert said.

"I hate to leave you shorthanded," Wally said.

"Think nothing of it, Wally," Robert said. "Your friends need your help. You can't exactly let them down now, can you?"

Wally looked at me. "I can go, Mr. Bekker," he said.

"We'll leave at ten o'clock from the White Plains airport," I said.

"I didn't know White Plains had an airport," Wally said. "Are you sure? Where is it located? Robert, did you know this?"

"I'll have a driver pick you up," Robert said. He shook my hand. "And thank you, Mr. Bekker," he said. "Thank you so very much."

"Oh boy," Regan said.

# Chapter Thirty-three

We took an Uber cab from White Plains to the Roosevelt Hotel on East 45th Street in Manhattan.

Campbell had reserved a suite for her and Regan, while I got a room down the hall.

After I dumped my bag on the bed, I walked down the hall and knocked on Campbell's door and Regan answered it.

"Dad, Campbell and I were just talking about you," she said.

"Oh?" I said.

"I'd like to take Regan shopping for a bit, and then I thought we'd take in a play," Campbell said.

"*Oh?*" I said and eyed Settina, who was asleep in her carrier beside the sofa.

"We'll be back around five to change," Campbell said. "Bottles are in the fridge with the schedule. Diapers are in the bag with the wipes. You have changed diapers before, haven't you?"

I looked at Campbell. "Favors owed have to be repaid," she said.

"Have a good time," I said.

The next four hours passed as slowly as if I had spent the entire time on a Stairmaster. Settina woke up twice in the first two hours, once for a bottle and again for a diaper change.

I watched a movie on television for the next two hours, and she woke up just once for a bottle and a changing.

Gratefully, Campbell and Regan returned on time at five o'clock.

Each had half a dozen shopping bags. I didn't ask what they bought.

"Bekker, we don't have to leave until seven-fifteen," Campbell said. "So if you want to use the hotel gym or whatever, go ahead. Just be back in time, we don't want to miss the opening curtain."

I went to my room and changed, then took the elevator to the third floor where the gym was located. As hotel gyms go, this one was decent, and I was able to get in a good hour before heading back to my room to shower.

I was back in Campbell's suite at seven.

Regan and Campbell wore new outfits that were comprised of black pants, white blouses and black jackets. Each wore matching, three-inch heels that elevated Regan to about five-foot-five inches tall.

"We'll be back at eleven," Campbell said. "You know the drill."

I watched another movie, fed and changed Settina twice, ordered a burger with fries and a pot of coffee from room service, and in between, I called Oz to check on Walt.

Elizabeth answered the phone.

"They're playing a video game," she said. "It involves a lot of car chases and things blowing up."

"But how does he seem?" I said.

"Surprisingly calm," Elizabeth said.

"Okay, I'll be home tomorrow," I said.

I surmised that "surprisingly calm" translated to Walt had accepted his fate and resigned himself to prison time.

I was surfing the cable channels on the television when Campbell and Regan arrived at eleven-fifteen.

The first thing they did was kick off their shoes. It was always amazing to me the pain women will endure to make their legs look better.

"Clive Owen was amazing," Regan said. "I didn't understand all of it, but he is so amazing. And gorgeous."

"I'll leave you to Clive and the dirty diapers," I said. "And see you for an early breakfast."

I had a difficult time falling asleep. "Surprisingly calm" kept creeping into my thoughts. I've known Walt since we went through the police academy together. I could use a lot of words to describe him, and the words surprisingly calm would never come to mind.

As a patrolman, Walt never made an easy arrest. As a detective, he was a bulldog and would never give up on a case. As lieutenant of detectives, he was a fair and honest boss who never asked his men to do anything he wouldn't.

Making captain of a precinct speaks for itself.

Fair, tough, thorough, intelligent, honest were words that came to mind concerning Walt.

Calm?

Never.

What was it they said when giving the weather and describing a pending storm? The calm before the storm.

The silence before the explosion.

I'd have to keep a close eye on him when we got home.

* * *

We reached the private airport by nine-thirty. While Carly and Regan boarded and settled in with Settina, I waited on the tarmac for Wally to arrive.

The Sample limo arrived fifteen minutes later, and a very disheveled looking Wally got out and looked at the waiting jetliner.

"We have a plane just like this one, but Robert doesn't let me ride on it," Wally said.

"Where's your luggage?" I said.

The driver opened the trunk and brought out a large suitcase.

"I don't like flying," Wally said.

I took the suitcase. "I know. You'll be fine," I said. "Let's go in and get you settled."

We boarded, and at the door, Wally said, "Not a lot of room in here."

"It seats twelve," I said. "A lot more room than on a…"

"Is that a baby Regan is holding?" Wally said.

"Hi, Wally. This is Settina." Regan said.

"When did you have a baby?" Wally said.

"Oh, no, see this is…" Regan said.

Campbell came out from the galley and looked at Wally.

"Oh boy." Wally said. "You're that pretty woman that's friends with that pretty lawyer-lady."

"Bekker, sit Wonder Boy down," Carly said. "We take off in five minutes."

"Come sit with me," Regan said.

Wally sat next to Regan.

"I don't like flying," Wally said.

"I know. Try to relax. It's a really smooth plane," Regan said.

Campbell took Settina and strapped her into the safety carrier, and then sat next to me and buckled up.

The plane started to roll forward.

"Here we go, here we go," Wally said. "We're going!"

Campbell glared at me.

The plane turned onto the runway.

Regan took Wally's hand.

"Oh boy, oh boy," Wally said. "We're really going."

Campbell turned and looked at Wally. "Yes, we really are going," she snapped.

The plane sped up, and with a massive thrust, we lifted off.

"Here we go, here we go," Wally said with eyes closed tight.

"For crying out loud, Bekker," Campbell said.

We climbed and leveled off, and Wally finally opened his eyes. "Where are we?" he said.

"In the clouds, Wally. We're in the clouds," Campbell said. She unbuckled, stood, and went to the galley.

I unbuckled and joined Campbell. She was making a pot of coffee.

"It's not Regan who is afraid of flying, it's that idiot genius," she said.

"Imagine him on a 757," I said.

"He takes the train home," Campbell said.

I returned to my seat. Wally was still holding Regan's hand. Campbell stuck her head out from the galley.

"I'm making coffee, would anyone care for a snack?" she said.

"Do you have any lettuce?" Wally said.

"Lettuce?" Campbell said.

Wally settled for a toasted bagel with cream cheese and coffee.

The flight was smooth, and Regan convinced Wally to watch a movie on the large screen television. They settled on a romantic comedy that had Wally sniffling and weeping, but at least he wasn't in a full blown panic attack.

Then the landing gear dropped, and Wally broke out in a sweat and gasped loudly.

"Here we go, here we go!" he proclaimed.

Campbell glared at me. "And we shall never go again," she said.

* * *

Wally and Regan sat in chairs in front of the bonfire in the trashcan while I grilled burgers and dogs.

"How difficult is it to do what Reed did in hacking into banks and business accounts and siphoning off money?" I said to Wally.

Wally was in the process of polishing his glasses on his shirt. He perched them back onto his nose and looked at me. "Close to impossible unless you're a genius," he said.

"Reed is," I said. "So how did he do it?"

"First, you'd need to hack into a system, which is almost impossible to do without being detected by a program designed to detect hackers," Wally said.

"What if you're the guy designing the systems for the banks and businesses?" I said.

"If I was the guy designing the systems to protect them, I would build in a back door access that only I could access undetected," Wally said. "I would use that back door to siphon off money into my account. See, interest rates and profits are usually rounded off because it's too much of a pain in the ass to deal with fractions of pennies. I would use my back door to gather up all these fractional pennies and no one would ever miss them."

"How would he spend this money?" I said. "Wouldn't it show up somewhere? Wouldn't the IRS pick up on it and investigate?"

"Not if you broke it up into many different accounts in many different banks," Wally said. "Accounts in foreign countries where numbers are used instead of names, out of reach of the IRS."

"The FBI recovered millions of dollars after they arrested him, but he could still have millions more squirreled away," I said.

"Which only he could access," Wally said.

"Through the programs only he knows about?" I said.

"Correct," Wally said.

"As part of his sentencing, he is never allowed to own a computer again," I said.

"Is he forbidden from using a computer at a library or having a girlfriend who owns one?" Wally said.

"No," I said.

"Then he's still in business," Wally said.

I flipped the burgers a final time and said, "Grab a plate."

"Do you have any…?" Wally said.

"Lettuce," Regan said. "I'll get it."

A few minutes later, as we ate burgers and dogs, we continued the conversation.

"So, Wally, say it was you," I said. "How would you…?"

"Say it was me what?" Wally said.

"Say you were Reed. How would you go about setting up Walt like he did?" I said.

"It wouldn't really be that difficult," Wally said. "I'd hack into the Depart of Motor Vehicles and steal all of his information. It isn't too hard to find somebody who makes fake licenses for illegals or felons and have one made up. The same guy could probably make you a passport. Then you fly to wherever and open an account at the bank in Captain Grimes's name."

"That's about how I see it," I said. "And you're going to help me catch him."

"Captain Grimes?" Wally said.

Regan rolled her eyes. "I think he means the bad guy, Wally," she said.

Wally nodded. "Any more lettuce?" he said.

# Chapter Thirty-four

After dropping Regan off at home, I drove Wally to Reed's mother's house. He had a laptop computer and told me to park directly across the street.

"The reason you see so many people sitting in their cars at libraries is because they're using the library's Wi-Fi. It's the same thing with coffee shops, hotels, and even a lot of gyms," Wally said. "So, if he has Wi-Fi, I should be able to tap into it."

After a few failed attempts, Wally shook his head no.

"I doubt he would use Wi-Fi where anybody could access it," Wally said.

"He wouldn't risk getting caught with a computer in the house, but I thought we'd check anyway," I said.

I drove to Riker's house and parked across the street. The house was dark, the 750i wasn't in the driveway, nor was the Jeep.

Wally checked his laptop and shook his head again.

I was about to start the engine when Wally said, "Wait. Look at that telephone pole. See the cable wires leading to the house? Two wires. One for electricity, the other is a cable wire. See?"

"I see them," I said.

"There's no phone line," Wally said. "Since they don't have Wi-Fi, the phone comes from the cable company. A bundle package. Phone, television, and Internet in one bundle package."

"So she might have a computer?" I said.

"It's hard to bundle a package without one," Wally said.

"What about a cell phone?" I said.

"Works off a tower," Wally said. "You don't need cable, Internet or Wi-Fi to have a cell phone."

"And she can send and receive emails from her phone?" I said.

"Text messages, most likely," Wally said.

"Could you hack her phone and computer?" I said.

"If I had a powerful enough computer, an IPO or a recent email address, I could do it," Wally said.

"I can get the computer you'd need, but the other two, no," I said.

"The FBI can tap a line in a matter of seconds," Wally said.

"Even the FBI needs a warrant, and they aren't likely to be on our side," I said.

"In the movies, a guy climbs the pole and taps the phone lines," Wally said.

"That's in the movies," I said. "And in the movies, the bad guys always miss and the good guy never gets hit."

I opened my door and Wally said, "How come your light didn't come on?"

"I disabled it for night work," I said. "Wait here, I'll be right back."

I crossed the street and followed the lines from the telephone pole around to the rear of the house. Several of the basement windows were painted black.

I returned to the car just as the 750i pulled into the driveway.

"Is that them?" Wally whispered.

"Yes," I said. "Now be quiet and still for a moment."

Reed and Riker exited the 750i and entered the house. Lights on the first floor came on, and then a light on the second floor in the front window came on.

"Sit tight for a second," I said.

I opened the car door and quietly got out, crossed the street, and checked the basement windows. The windows that weren't painted black were lit up.

I returned to the car.

"He's in the basement, probably on the computer," I said.

I started the engine and drove back to the trailer.

* * *

Wally sipped ginger ale from a can and watched the fire in the trashcan glow.

"I'll need something custom made," he said. "Is there a private dealer in town that makes computers from scratch?"

"I don't know, but I'll find out," I said.

"I could use a snack," Wally said. "I think better when I eat."

We went inside where I toasted some bagels.

As we munched buttered bagels, Wally looked at the computer I bought in town.

"Standard," Wally said. "Nothing a real hacker would use. Not enough drive or memory."

"We'll see about getting you what you need," I said.

Wally bit into a bagel. "Were you scared tonight? I was," he said.

"No, Wally, I wasn't scared," I said. "And neither should you be."

Wally nodded. "We need to find a dealer who can make a computer that suits our needs," he said.

"I'm sure we'll find one," I said.

"Wait," Wally said. He turned to the computer and started searching and then said, "There."

I looked at the screen. Custom-made PC's and computer repair. Jake's Computer World.

"Do you know where this is?" Wally said.

I looked at the address. "I know exactly where it is," I said.

"I'm going to bed," Wally said.

"Good idea," I agreed.

* * *

"I want the most powerful hard drive you have in the store," Wally told Jake.

Jake looked at Wally. "That's a nine thousand dollar drive," he said.

"And your biggest flat monitor, top of the line speakers, and best keyboard," Wally said.

"Don't be insulted, friend, but you're talking about twelve thousand dollars worth of equipment here," Jake said.

I was about to interrupt when Wally opened his wallet and tossed his corporate gold card on the counter.

Jake looked at it.

"It's good," Wally said. "Check it if you like."

"Well, let's get started," Jake said.

While Wally and Jake played around with computer equipment, I went outside and called Carly.

"How's it going?" I said.

"We're working on subpoenas and suppressions," Carly said. "Where are you?"

"Outside a strip mall with Wally," I said.

"What the hell are you doing there?" Carly said.

"Shopping," I said. "I'll tell you about it later. From here, I'm going to see Walt."

"Tell him to stay calm," Carly said. "We'll be by to see him tomorrow."

I hung up and called Jane.

"I see you survived traveling with Wally," she said.

"He's better, actually," I said.

"Better than what?" Jane said.

"Better than before," I said. "So listen, he's staying with me for a few days, so…"

"At the trailer?"

"Yes."

"So, come over to my house."

"And leave him alone?"

"He's forty years old, for God's sake," Jane said.

"He can barely tie the laces on his sneakers," I said. "But, I'll see what I can do."

"Call me later," Jane said.

I hung up and returned to the store where Wally and Jake were testing some kind of super computer at the counter.

"This is the one," Wally said. "Pack it up, Jake, we'll take it."

* * *

While Wally assembled the new super brain on the kitchen table, I changed and got in a workout on the heavy and speed bags and push-up bars.

By the time I was done, Wally was putting his new toy through its paces.

"Give me an hour to program what I'll need," he said.

I went for a run and when I returned, Wally was on one of the social media sites.

"What's her full name, the girlfriend?" Wally said.

"Rosamund Rose Riker," I said.

"Unusual name," Wally said. "Well, let's see what we see."

While Wally was seeing, I grabbed a shower. By the time I reemerged fully dressed, he was lost in thought.

He was so engrossed in what he was doing, he didn't notice as I made a pot of coffee and took a mug to the table.

"Wally?" I said.

He reached for my mug and took a sip. I got up and filled another mug and then sat down again.

"Wally, what are you doing?" I said.

"Oh, see, I'm looking at her profile page," Wally said as he took another sip from the mug.

I scooted around and looked at the giant monitor. The profile page on the social network site was for Rosamund Rose Riker.

"People are so stupid when it comes to their personal information," Wally said. "She listed her email address under contact information."

"Can you use that?" I said.

"It's like the combination to a safe, if you know how," Wally said. "I once spent three weeks hacking into the computer systems of a Vegas casino just to gain the odds on March Madness, and they had a firewall you wouldn't believe."

"Does she have a firewall?" I said.

"Everybody does," Wally said. "And most are useless against a pro hacker. The United States Government has the best programs available, and they still get hacked all the time."

"But they know they're being hacked and shut it down," I said.

"And they just get hacked again," Wally said. "It's the time between when they get hacked and shut it down where all the damage is done. It's like a game to these people. Some hackers do it just for the fun of doing it."

"All that aside, can you hack into her computer and see if Reed is using it?" I said.

Wally looked at the monitor and nodded. "Is there any coffee?" he said.

"Besides the mug at your fingertips?" I said.

"I'd love some," Wally said as he tapped some keys.

# Chapter Thirty-five

While Wally toiled over the computer, I took a drive to visit Walt. He was in the backyard playing ring toss with Regan.

"Give us a few minutes, honey," I told Regan.

"I'll make you some coffee," Regan said and went inside.

"How are things in Wally World?" Walt said.

"He's actually calmed down quite a bit since last year," I said.

We took chairs at the patio table.

"And you needed him because…?" Walt asked.

"He's going to help me get to the bottom of all this," I said.

"We are talking about the same Wally Sample?" Walt said.

"He's a crackpot for sure, but he's also a genius," I said.

"Do I even want to know what you're up to?" Walt said.

"No, but that's not why I'm here," I said. "I'm just checking up on my oldest friend is all."

"Am I on suicide watch now?" Walt said.

"I just want to know what you're thinking, Walt," I said.

Regan appeared with two mugs of coffee.

"Thank you, honey," Walt said.

"Dad, Aunt Liz and I are going grocery shopping," Regan said. "Is there anything special you'd like, Uncle Walt?"

"Ice cream. A quart of chocolate ice cream," Walt said.

"That's it?" Regan said.

"Liz knows everything else."

Regan nodded and went back inside.

Walt sipped from his mug and then looked at me. "I'm not going to off myself, Jack, if that's what you're worried about," he said. "I've resigned myself to the fact I'm going to do some time. How much, how little, doesn't really matter. I'll lose my pension and that leaves Liz without an income. Our daughters aren't really established enough to be of much help. I told her to sell the house and get a small place, or move in with one of our daughters. The house is worth three-fifty, maybe four hundred thousand in today's market."

"That won't happen," I said. "You have my word on it. That will *not* happen."

"Why, what are you going to do?" Walt said.

"Finish my coffee, and then go back and see what Wally is up to," I said.

Walt sighed. "I really don't want you for a cellmate, Jack," he said.

"Relax. Watch a movie with Oz or something," I said. "I'll stop by tomorrow with Carly and Kagan."

I left Walt at the patio table and went in to see Oz. He walked out with me to the car.

"Anything I should know about?" Oz said.

"How is it going with the real estate developer?" I said.

"We got thirty days left before he kicks us out," Oz said. "I got an appointment to look at design plans next week. You coming?"

"Let me know where and when," I said.

Oz gave me his look. "Whatever you're up to, give me fair warning," he said. "I have Regan, the cat, and the damn dog to think about."

"I'll see you tomorrow," I said. "Carly and Kagan are stopping by. I'll grill up some lunch."

* * *

Wally, dressed in a robe, was in the lounge chair when I arrived at the trailer. He had taped two sheets of aluminum foil to cardboard he had cut from the box the computer was packed in, and was using them to tan his face.

I grabbed the chair next to him.

"I used her email to track her IPO address. I was going to…" Wally said.

"IPO?" I said.

"Every computer has an address built in," Wally said. "It's how the FBI can track a pervert to a computer. Like with that congressman who was emailing pictures of his privates to underage girls. Some people are just sick, I guess. A grown man sending perverted pictures to a fifteen-year-old girl. That reminds me of a gambler I knew back in Vegas who…"

"Wally, about this IPO?" I said.

"Oh, right, see, what I can do now that I have the IPO is take control of the computer as if it was my own," Wally said. "I can check emails, bank accounts, everything that computer was ever used for."

"Deleted stuff?" I said.

"Nothing is ever really deleted if you know where to find it," Wally said.

"So, why are you out here with tinfoil on your face instead of working on the computer?" I said.

"Somebody logged on, so I logged off," Wally said.

"You can see that?" I said.

"And they can see me," Wally said. "So I shut down."

"Get dressed," I said. "We're going to dinner."

* * *

"I thought you said we were going to dinner," Wally said.

"We are," I said.

We were parked across the street from Riker's house. Reed's 750i was parked in the driveway. Light was coming from the front basement windows.

"Alright, let's go," I said.

I drove to the greasy spoon diner, a small restaurant not far from the beach. The place lived up to its name, serving the messiest, greasiest bacon burgers anywhere. We ordered the burger plate special with bowls of chili on the side.

Wally requested extra lettuce with his.

"Clear a few things up for me," I said as I ate a French fry. "You can log in and take control of Riker's computer?"

"It isn't that difficult to do if you have the IPO address," Wally said. "Computer repair companies and service providers do it all the time if a customer has a problem they can't fix."

"And you can operate the computer as if it was your own?" I said.

"That's the point," Wally said.

"But, if he's logged on, he can also see you?" I said.

"Through a little window or pop up box that tells him someone else is logged in and is in control," Wally said.

"So, you can only operate when we know nobody is using Riker's computer?" I said.

Wally bit into his burger, nodded, and wiped grease off his chin with a paper napkin.

"We'll have to work around it," I said. "Early morning or late at night, maybe even afternoon."

"Exactly what do you want me to do?" Wally said.

"This son of a bitch set Walt up with six hundred thousand dollars," I said, "after he got out of prison. He has money the FBI never found. I want to you find that money."

"Just find it?" Wally said.

I looked at Wally.

"You mean steal it?" Wally said.

"Transfer it to me, so I have total control," I said. "Then you go home and forget it ever happened."

"But what's he going to do when his money goes missing?" Wally said.

"I can tell you what he *isn't* going to do, and that is report it to the police," I said.

After we left the diner, I drove back to Riker's house. It was dark and the 750i was gone.

"We might have a couple of hours for you to work," I said.

* * *

I was in my chair in front of a bonfire in the trashcan. Wally was inside working on the computer. It was a moonless night and the beach was pitch-black. I could hear the gentle lapping of the surf about a hundred yards away, but it was impossible to see.

Around midnight, a bleary-eyed Wally emerged and plunked down in the chair beside me.

"I isolated one foreign bank account," he said. "A numbered account in the First Bank of Zurich. That's in Switzerland."

"I know."

"You'd be surprised how many people think it's in Germany because of the name," Wally said.

"For how much?" I said.

"How much what?"

"Money in the account?"

"One million even," Wally said.

"Good work, Wally, but there's more," I said. "You can bet on it."

"I'm tired," Wally said. "I'm going to bed."

"Go, you earned it," I said.

Wally stood, nodded, and went back inside.

I sat for a while until my eyes grew heavy, and then I went inside for some much needed sleep.

# Chapter Thirty-six

I was up before dawn, took coffee in my chair, and watched the horizon slowly lighten over the ocean.

The thing I would miss the most about having the trailer on the beach would be the sunrise and sunset.

We could have it again if we purchased a condo, but it wouldn't be the same sharing it with two dozen other units.

By the second cup of coffee, the early orange sun was on my face and Wally was awake.

He stumbled out wearing his robe and holding a mug of coffee. He plopped into a chair beside me and said, "I heard you get up."

"I'll make breakfast," I said. "What would you like?"

"Maybe some bacon and eggs."

"Over easy?"

Wally nodded. "I think I'll check and see if it's safe to work," he said.

While Wally fooled around with the computer, I fixed breakfast. Eggs over easy, bacon, hash browns, toast and orange juice.

We ate at the kitchen table.

"I'm close to locating another account," Wally said.

"Under his real name?"

"From years ago. It sat dormant for a very long time."

"How do you transfer the funds to me?" I said.

"Set up numbered accounts at banks and transfer the funds," Wally said. "The banks won't even realize it's been done right under their noses."

"And it's all numbered accounts?"

Wally nodded.

"And I'll be able to access them?"

"Just use the numbers to authorize access."

"Besides using Riker's computer to access his accounts, is Reed doing anything else?" I said.

"If you mean emails, no," Wally said. "But, I did find that he's transferred ten thousand dollars a month into Riker's checking account, and five thousand a month into his mother's checkbook. He's doing it in weekly increments to avoid detection."

"Does he have an account locally for himself?" I said.

"I haven't found that yet," Wally said.

"See what you can do before noon," I said. "We're having lunch at my house."

* * *

Wally isolated a second numbered account in the Bank of London in Grand Cayman. It was located just a few blocks from the bank Cena managed. There was a transaction for a six hundred thousand dollar withdrawal the same day Walt's account was opened.

Reed withdrew the money, walked a few blocks, and opened the account.

The account in the Bank of London showed a balance of four hundred thousand dollars.

Reed liked even numbers. His computer-logged, genius brain was probably wired that way.

My guess was that his other accounts would balance out at a million apiece.

Wally still hadn't located a local account for Reed. He was living off the five thousand a month he put into his mother's checking account.

He was living low and off the radar. For now. My guess was he would wait until Walt's trial, and then disappear with his millions, leaving his mother behind, possibly taking Riker with him.

We left the trailer around eleven-thirty, and I drove to the big grocery store in town and then to my house.

Carly and Kagan were already there when we arrived. Kagan wore slacks and a polo shirt. Carly was informally dressed in shorts, a sleeveless blouse and tennis sneakers.

Oz, Regan and Elizabeth were in the living room while Carly, Kagan and Walt sat at the patio table in the backyard.

I joined the group at the patio table.

"We got a trial date in the state supreme court," Carly said. "It's set for two months and two weeks from today."

"Napier as first chair?" I said.

Carly nodded. "I'm sure he'll have at least two top ADAs assisting him at trial," she said.

Kagan looked at me. "And what have you been up to?" he said. "With your little friend there."

"Lunch," I said.

I went to the rear of the patio and fired up the four-burner grill. While it heated up, I lowered the retractable patio awning to shade the table.

Carly and Kagan continued talking to Walt and making notes.

I went into the kitchen and brought out a large platter of steak tips, chicken breasts and thighs. As the tips and chicken sizzled, Kagan wandered over to me.

"Jack, what are you doing?" he said.

"Grilling," I said.

"With the little man in there?" Kagan said.

"He's helping me with research," I said.

"Research, huh?"

The grill had a side burner for warming a pot of baked beans. "Keep an eye on this for a minute," I said.

I returned to the kitchen and brought out the pot of baked beans and set it onto the warmer.

Kagan was puffing on a cigar and blew a cloud of grey smoke. "I know how you get, Jack," he said. "When something takes root in that brain of yours, you don't let it go, no matter what."

"Frank, if there was something to tell, I would tell you," I said. "Ask Regan to bring out the plates, would you?"

We ate at the table, and it seemed more like a family gathering than a pretrial meeting of the minds.

Regan and Elizabeth baked a lemon cake for dessert and served it with ice cream and coffee.

Afterward, Carly and Kagan continued their meeting with Walt.

Oz told me we had a meeting on Tuesday at noon with the real estate developer. Then Wally and I drove back to the trailer. Along the way, we swung past Riker's house and no one was home.

At the trailer, Wally logged in and went to work.

While he worked, I took a long workout and then jogged along the water.

By five o'clock, we both were exhausted.

Wally had located three accounts in Reed's name, totaling two million, four hundred thousand dollars. We knew they weren't being drawn upon as they hadn't been accessed in nine years.

"What do you plan to do with all this when we're finished?" Wally said.

"Bring the entire mess to the FBI and have Walt cleared and reinstated," I said.

"Won't they want to know how you came by all this?" Wally said.

"I'm sure they will," I said.

"What are you going to tell them?"

"Certainly nothing about you," I said. "I'll frame it so they can take the credit."

"I'm tired. I think I'm done for today," Wally said.

"Relax," I said. "I'm going to do some surveillance work, but you can take it easy until I get back."

"Maybe you can drop me off at your house, and I can hang out there until you get back?" Wally said.

"Sure."

* * *

I parked at the corner and watched Reed's mother's house. The Ford was in the driveway, and the lights were on inside.

Shortly after dark, Reed emerged from the house, retrieved the 750i from the garage and took off.

I gave him plenty of room and drove to Riker's house where the 750i was in the driveway by the time I arrived.

I parked diagonally across the street.

Lights came on in the basement.

Reed was on the computer.

I decided to give it an hour. My patience was rewarded when Reed and Riker emerged from the house, got into the 750i and Riker drove off.

I called it a night and drove to my house.

Walt, Oz and Elizabeth were playing cards at the patio table under the light from the floodlights. They were drinking lemonade.

Regan and Wally were playing a video game on television.

I went outside and sat at the table. Elizabeth poured me a glass of lemonade.

"Want to play a few hands?" Oz said.

"Take my place," Elizabeth said. "I'll bring out some cake and coffee."

A little while later, Regan and Wally joined us, and we finished off the lemon cake from lunch and washed it down with coffee.

Before Wally and I left, I spoke privately with Walt in the backyard.

"The trial's gonna be rough on Elizabeth and our daughters," Walt said.

"Elizabeth is stronger than you think," I said.

"That prick Napier sent over a plea deal, did you know that?" Walt said.

"I didn't."

"Ten to fifteen with a parole option after seven and full loss of my pension," Walt said.

"You're not seriously considering that?" I said.

"Out in seven, I'm still young enough to be of some use to Elizabeth," Walt said.

"But you didn't do it," I said. "What do Carly and Kagan say?"

"If it was a slam dunk, there wouldn't be an offer on the table," Walt said.

"Listen to them," I said. "A plea is off the table."

"If I lose, I'm gone for life," Walt said.

"You're not going to lose," I said. "Like you said, if it was a slam dunk, they wouldn't have offered a plea."

Walt nodded.

"I got to take Wally home and put him to bed before Regan adopts him as the big brother she never had," I said.

# Chapter Thirty-seven

Jane and I were sitting on the edge of the water while Regan tossed a tennis ball to her pug.

Behind us, Oz sat in his chair with Molly on his lap.

Jane reached for her cigarette case and lit one with a disposable lighter.

"So what is Young Frankenstein working on in there?' she said.

"Research," I said.

"Don't give me that crap, Jack," Jane said. "You and the big brain are cooking something up concerning Walt. I'd like to know what it is in case I have to arrest you for it down the road."

"You'll just have to trust me," I said.

"Famous last words," Jane said. "In fact, I heard those exact words just before I caught my ex in bed with a nineteen-year-old."

I looked out at the ocean. A few sailboats dotted the horizon, along with a cruise ship.

"We're, or should I say, Wally is trying to figure out how Reed set Walt up," I said. "And we're close."

"Jesus Christ, Jack," Jane said. "Has it ever occurred to you that you're breaking the law and could wind up as Walt's cellmate?"

"No," I said.

"Well, it should," Jane said. "And as your house is in the county limits, I'd be the one to have to lock you up. I wouldn't like that, Bekker. Not at all."

"It wouldn't exactly thrill me either," I said. "But, if that happens, you can still keep the earrings."

Jane looked at me. I could see the fury building in her eyes. Her nostrils flared, her lips tightened into a thin, tense line.

"Or not," I said.

I watched as her right hand balled into a tight fist.

Before she took her shot, I stood up. "I think I'll go for a run," I said.

"Run, Forest, run," Jane called after me.

I jogged for about thirty minutes and when I returned, Jane and Regan were tossing a Frisbee. As I walked past them, the Frisbee hit me on the back of the head.

"Did you hear that echo, Regan?" Jane said. "Empty as a balloon."

Wally was in a chair beside Oz. Molly was still on Oz's lap, but now the pug was on Wally's lap.

"I need to show you something," Wally said.

"Show," I said.

I followed Wally into the trailer and closed the door.

"I had to log off because she logged on," Wally said.

"How do you know it was Riker?" I said.

"The first thing she did was go to her email," Wally said. "I shut down, but I started a file with screenshots. Have a look."

Wally opened the file that contained four screenshots. He located a fourth account in Zurich that had two million dollars in it.

"You have the account numbers for all four?" I said.

"I wrote them down," Wally said.

"Which account is he using to finance Riker and his mother?"

"The same one he used to withdraw the six hundred thousand."

I looked at the screenshots. "There's more," I said.

Wally looked at me and nodded.

"You're not going to find them today," I said. "We might as well have some fun while we can."

We went outside. Jane and Regan were in the water. Oz was in his chair with Molly still on his lap. The pug was at the shoreline, barking at Regan.

"Wally, come in the water," Regan yelled to Wally.

"I don't have trunks," Wally said.

"Grab a pair of mine in the closet."

Wally went back inside. I took my chair next to Oz.

"I'm not so sure I want to see that boy in a bathing suit," Oz said.

A few minutes passed, and then the trailer door opened. "It's a little big," Wally said.

"Let's have a look," I said.

Wally stepped out wearing a pair of my trunks. They ended close to his ankles. His white belly hung over the waistband. His chest was as pale as a glass of milk.

Oz stared at him.

"I feel ridiculous," Wally said.

"You look… fine," I said.

"I look like the ghost of a Weeble," Wally said.

"No, you look good," Oz said.

"Wally, come on!" Regan called out.

Wally cautiously walked past us and down to the water.

"Good lord," Oz said.

"Wally's value is in his brain, not his looks," I said.

"That boy is proof God has a sense of humor," Oz said.

After lunch, Jane and I took a walk along the beach.

She held my hand with her left hand and smoked a cigarette with her right.

"Talk to me, Jack," she said. "You owe me that much, seeing as how it was my department that arrested Smith, and Walt is in my care."

I took the cigarette from Jane, inhaled, and gave it back to her.

"What we're doing isn't legal," I said. "You could be implicated if you know about it and did nothing."

Jane looked at me as she inhaled on the cigarette. "What you said earlier about bringing down Reed, you're using Wally to build a case against him to do what?"

"Prove Walt is innocent," I said.

"And if the proof is obtained illegally, what good is it?" Jane asked as she exhaled smoke through her nose. "Unless you're willing to take a hit and go down for it."

I took the cigarette and inhaled and gave it back to Jane.

"You are, aren't you?" Jane said. "You stupid son of a bitch."

"I never claimed to be smart," I said. "Just loyal."

"I'll give you that, Jack," Jane said. "But if your dumb ass winds up in my jail, how loyal are you to Regan?"

I stopped walking and looked at Jane.

She tossed the cigarette away. "Or me?" she said.

"If I see things go sour, I'll bring the whole thing to you and let the court settle it out," I said. "But let me take my turn at bat first."

Jane nodded. "I'll be there when you strike out," she said.

* * *

Around nine o'clock, Wally logged on and deemed it safe to continue working. I made a fire in the trashcan, drank coffee, and thought about what I was doing.

Jane was right when she said what I was doing was illegal and would be useless in court, if it came to that. I could get three years for violating the hacking laws, if it came to that.

Wally could get the same, if it came to that.

I would have to make sure that it didn't.

Around midnight I went inside and found Wally asleep at the table.

I shook his arm and he opened his eyes. "Oh, Mr. Bekker, I must have fallen asleep," he said.

I glanced at the monitor. "What do you got?" I said.

"Account numbers five and six, each with two million dollars in them," Wally said.

"Go to bed, Wally," I said. "Tomorrow is another day."

Wally logged off, then stood, yawned, and went to his bedroom.

I closed and locked the door, then went to my bedroom and tried to grab some sleep.

Jane's words echoed around in my mind.

"I'll be there when you strike out," she said.

Not good words to fall asleep by.

# Chapter Thirty-eight

Three days later, Wally found a seventh account in a bank in Switzerland. It had two million dollars in it that hadn't been drawn upon in nine-plus years.

On Tuesday, Oz, Regan and I met the real estate developer in his office and looked at his drawings of the condo proposal. We selected the last condo, a four-bedroom, two-bathroom deluxe that had a backyard and a front patio facing the ocean. We made arrangements to close on the deal a few weeks down the road.

Wally worked tirelessly.

I sat around a lot and thought.

Reed used his time in prison to plot and plan his revenge, and recruit Smith to help him once he was back on the outside.

He recruited Riker to supply the computer he needed to enact his revenge, which, to this point, was going according to plan.

If you ever played chess, you knew the key to winning the game was to anticipate your opponent's moves before he made them and to have a counter strategy in place.

I wondered what Reed's plan was for after Walt's trial and conviction.

Would he stick around and continue to live low with his mother and girlfriend?

I doubted that.

My guess was Reed would take off for Europe and live high off his money. He would leave his mother taken care of, but Smith and Riker were witnesses to his handiwork.

He could take Riker with him and always dispose of her in the Swiss Alps somewhere.

Smith, not so much.

Smith was a cheap crook who would want more and probably blackmail Reed to get it.

Conclusion: Reed would have to dispose of Smith.

After Smith testified at the trial, of course.

It didn't really matter at this point if Wally found additional accounts, I had enough to take to the FBI, but some additional gravy would be nice.

I gave Wally a few extra days, and he located two more accounts, bringing the total to nine, with collectively just short of fifteen million dollars.

* * *

Wally was asleep at the kitchen table when I entered the trailer. I gently shook him awake.

"Wally, it's time for you to go home," I said.

"Right now?"

"Day after tomorrow," I said. "Right now, go get some sleep."

Wally logged off the computer and stumbled his way to the bedroom.

I sat and thought for a while. When my eyes grew heavy, I went to my bedroom, and for once, fell asleep within minutes.

* * *

In the morning, Wally talked me through everything, and I took extensive notes concerning accounts and activity, including the numbered codes needed to access each account. I had screenshots of it all in a thick file that I locked up in my file cabinet.

Then I drove home to pick up Regan and Oz for a final, farewell cookout with Wally.

It was a hot day, and Wally and Regan played in the water while I worked the grill, and Oz sat in his chair with the cat on his lap.

The ever-present pug begged for scraps at my ankles.

"The genius goes home tomorrow?" Oz said.

"By train," I said. "He doesn't want to fly commercial."

"When your plan blows up in your face, what happens to him?" Oz said.

"What plan, and I thought you didn't care about him," I said.

"What plan? Whatever crazy scheme you brought him here to help you concoct. *That* plan," Oz said. "And I never say I didn't care about him, I said… oh never mind. Go on and get yourself locked up, or worse. See if I care about your dumb ass."

"How many burgers and dogs do you want?" I said.

"One of each," Oz said.

"Baked beans?"

"Yeah, baked beans. You been grilling me the same shit for fifteen years, you need to ask?" Oz said.

"Remember your blood pressure," I said.

"My blood pressure fine, it's you the real pain in my ass," Oz said. "And you gonna get that boy hurt, or worse."

"He goes home in the morning," I said. "And he has nothing to do with anything."

Oz looked down at the water where Regan was laughing at something Wally had said or done.

"She don't go home in the morning," Oz said.

"I just need a couple more days," I said.

Oz sighed and patted Molly. "How's them dogs coming?" he said.

* * *

"When you get home, none of this ever happened," I said. "If by some chance it does happen to come up, I asked you to help me build a computer for my business, and you were nice enough to take the time to teach me. That's all you know."

Wally looked at me over his bowl of soup. We were at a restaurant in town, having a last meal together before he took the train home in the morning.

I reached into my jacket pocket for my checkbook and removed one for twelve thousand dollars and slid it across the table.

"For the computer," I said.

"Mr. Bekker, you don't have to…" Wally said.

"It's my computer," I said. "You just taught me how to use it, and it's perfectly fine to call me Jack like everybody else does."

Wally continued to look at me over his bowl of soup.

"Wally, please don't cry," I said.

* * *

In the morning, I drove Wally to the Amtrak station and waited with him on the platform.

"Mr. Bekker… I mean, Jack, I don't know what to say," Wally said as the train arrived.

I extended my right hand and Wally reached out and hugged me.

"Okay, Wally, alright," I said.

"I'll come visit," Wally said.

"Sure, anytime," I said.

Sniffling, Wally boarded the train and the doors closed.

# Chapter Thirty-nine

I sat in my chair and made notes on a legal pad. I needed to bring Paul Lawrence into the fold and get him to open a case file against Reed.

My inbox list of favors was short and growing shorter.

The outgoing was long and growing longer by the minute.

I put everything away and went for a jog along the water. When I returned, the heavy bag got a thirty-minute workout, followed by the speed bag and push-up bars.

I used the time to let my thoughts wander, and when I was finished with the last push-up, I was ready to swallow my pride and call Paul Lawrence.

After a quick shower, I made some coffee, took my chair and called Paul in Washington.

I was transferred twice before I was connected to his office. Then I got his voicemail box.

"Paul, it's John Bekker," I said. "I know you said you didn't want a heads up, but I have some vital information for you. Critical for Walt. Call me back when you get this."

The afternoon passed without Paul returning my call.

Jane showed up around six o'clock.

She bounced out of her cruiser, removing her holster as she walked.

"Who died?" she said.

"Nobody, I'm just waiting," I said.

"Your wait's over, I'm here," Jane said.

She placed the holster on the table and sat on my lap.

"One word about my weight gets you a black eye," she said.

"Wally went home this morning," I said.

"And you're sad because you lost your little pet?"

"I'm relieved he's no longer a part of this," I said.

Jane stood up from my lap. "I'm grabbing a shower to wash the stink of today's prisoners off me," she said. "If you'd care to join me, perhaps I can show you a few things that might cheer you up a bit."

She snatched her holster and sashayed into the trailer, and nobody could sashay like Jane.

* * *

Around one in the morning, I woke up, untangled myself from Jane's hair and legs, and went to the kitchen for a glass of milk.

I sat at the table and looked at the dark monitor as I sipped. I had yet to turn the computer on myself, and had no plans to anytime soon.

Halfway through the milk, a naked and sleepy Jane wandered into the kitchen.

"What is it?" she said.

"Milk."

"I mean, why are you awake?"

"Because I couldn't sleep."

Jane took the glass from my hand, took a small sip and set it on the table. Then she sat on my lap.

"This," she said and wiggled on top of me, "is more effective than this," she said and touched the glass of milk, "for a good night's sleep."

Who was I to argue?

* * *

In the morning after Jane left for work, I called Paul Lawrence again and again, and I was shifted over to his voicemail. Again.

"Paul, it's Jack. I know I'm being a pain in the ass, but I have something for you concerning Walt," I said. "Pease call me back."

I wasted the morning, made a light lunch, and then started the afternoon with a workout on the heavy bag.

Between the heavy bag and speed bag, Carly called.

"Bekker, where have you been?" Carly said.

"Research."

"Come on, Jack, don't feed me that crap," Carly said.

"I'll fill you in when I'm positive," I said.

"The limo is on the way to pick you up. We're having a meeting with the trial judge at three this afternoon," Carly said. "Evidence hearing."

"I'll brush off my suit," I said.

"Better yet, buy a new one," Carly said. "And maybe a tie that isn't twenty years old and came out of a thrift shop."

* * *

The trial judge was the Honorable Andrew J. Foss, a man who sat on the bench for twenty-plus years after a career as a state prosecutor. His reputation was one of being fair but strict, a no nonsense judge who didn't tolerate grandstanding from either side in his courtroom.

Carly and Kagan met with Napier outside the courtroom before Foss was ready to see us.

"Are you ready to surrender, Carly, or are you letting your captain take a twenty-five-year fall?" Napier sneered.

"Are you offering another deal?" Carly said.

"The People are not without heart, Carly," Napier said. "Seven to ten with parole after five. This offer is off the table after today."

"Worried your case is weak?" Kagan said.

"No deal," Carly said. "We wouldn't even consider it unless it's three to seven, parole after three."

"You're dreaming," Napier said.

The door to Foss's chambers opened and a court deputy said, "Judge Foss will see you now."

The meeting lasted about ninety minutes. Foss heard all of the evidence. He wasn't a happy judge with some of it.

The testimony of Smith and Cena was borderline, in his opinion, and he considered the reports from Travis to be grandstanding.

"I won't allow my courtroom to be turned into a three ring circus," Foss said. "By the People *or* the defense. Is that clear to everyone in this room?"

It was.

"Have the People offered a plea to the defense?" Foss said.

"Yes, and it was rejected, your honor," Napier said.

Foss looked at Carly and Kagan. "Well, we have a rodeo then," he said. "Jury selection will begin in thirty days."

That's when Kagan tossed a monkey wrench into the works.

"Your honor, the defense requests a change of venue," Kagan said.

"On what grounds?" Napier snapped.

"There isn't a single person in this state who hasn't been prejudiced against my client by the publicity of his arrest," Kagan said. "How are we supposed to pick an unbiased jury from a contaminated pool?"

Foss looked at Napier. "Ball's in your court, Mr. Napier," he said.

"Where and who presides?" Napier said.

"I'll contact you by the end of the week," Foss said. "Is there anything else?"

* * *

The limo took us to my house to meet with Walt and give him the latest news.

"Change of venue? To where?" he asked.

"We don't know yet, but it buys us additional time," Carly said.

"Napier had an epiphany and offered us another plea," Kagan said. "He must have realized a trial might bring different results than a grand jury hearing."

"What was the offer this time?" Walt said.

"Seven to ten, parole after five," Carly said.

Walt nodded. "You turned it down?"

"Of course," Carly said. "We can beat them and they know it, or they wouldn't have made another offer."

"What if I lose?" Walt said.

"Don't even think that way," Carly said. "Because you won't."

Walt looked at me. "Jack?"

"She's right, don't even think that way," I said.

"We're going to be a while, Jack. Do you want the limo to take you back or will you be staying here?" Carly said.

"Back," I said.

* * *

I called Paul Lawrence and again got his voicemail.

I left another message, and when he didn't call back by ten in the evening, I made it an early night and went to bed, half-hoping Paul would call. When he didn't, I stared at the black ceiling waiting for sleep that was a long time coming.

# Chapter Forty

Scratching at the door woke me up. I opened my eyes and listened in the dark for a few seconds. The noise I heard was someone picking the lock on the front door.

I rolled to my left, quietly opened the drawer on the nightstand, and removed the Kimber .45 pistol I kept there. It wasn't loaded as I had the magazines in the bottom drawer. I opened it, grabbed a seven round magazine, inserted it and racked the slide.

Then I walked quietly to the kitchen and stood to the left of the door.

I listened to the lock click open and the doorknob turn.

It opened and a man with a flashlight slowly walked in. Directly behind him was a second man.

I let the first man get far enough in for me to hit him on the back of the head with the .45 and as he went down, I grabbed the man behind him and clubbed him across the jaw.

I stepped over the fallen two, rushed outside and peered into the dark at another man running towards town.

He had a big lead and a bird in hand and all that, so I went back inside and called the sheriff's department.

* * *

By the time two county cruisers, plus Jane in her own cruiser arrived, I had the fallen two hogtied on the floor with rope.

"What the fuck, Bekker?" Jane said as she and four deputies

piled into the trailer.

I was at the table with a glass of milk. "Ask them," I said.

The deputies yanked them to their feet, frisked them and found a set of lock picks, but no weapons.

"Who the fuck would want to rob your dump, Bekker?" Jane said.

"Ask them," I said.

* * *

We sorted it all out in Jane's interrogation room. The two stooges, minus the one who got away, were a small time B&E crew. They usually worked homes and apartments after they scouted them for alarms and dogs.

Both had long records that were about to get longer.

Their story was as follows: they usually scout their own jobs, but a man approached them at the bar they use for a hangout and offered them five thousand dollars to ransack his trailer.

"*His* trailer?" Jane said.

"That's what he said," the man I hit first said. "His trailer. He said it was an insurance thing."

"He said 'take everything of value and burn it,'" the second man said.

"He paid you in cash?" Jane said.

"Yeah, cash," the first man said.

"Did you get his name?" Jane asked.

"He called himself Bekker," the second man said.

"Just Bekker?" Jane said.

"That's what he said," the second man replied.

"What did he look like?" Jane said.

"Maybe six-foot-two. He wore sunglasses and a wool hat," The first man said. "And the bar was dark."

Jane looked at the two deputies against the wall. "Book them, then call the PD office and have them arraigned in the morning."

Jane and I went to her office.

"You pissed somebody off, Jack," Jane said. "Now is a good time to fill me in."

"Are you asking as the sheriff or as my lady?" I said.

"As the sheriff it's my job, as your lady it's my concern," Jane said.

"The answer is I have no idea," I said.

Jane stared at me. "Three clowns are hired to rob and burn your shithole trailer and you have no idea?" she said.

"None."

Jane sat behind her desk and lit a cigarette. "Lucky for you I was pulling a double today, because I'm too damn tired to kick your ass up and down the hallway," she said.

"So you're not holding me?" I said.

"I'll hold you later when I see you," Jane said.

I nodded and turned to the door.

"Nice Kimber, by the way," Jane said.

"It was a gift from Walt for my birthday a few years back," I said.

* * *

The sun was up by the time I returned to the trailer. A gift bag was on my chair. I picked it up and removed the tissue paper.

I pulled out the quart bottle of Ballantine's seventeen-year-old scotch from the bag and looked at it.

In the sun, the liquid glowed a deep amber.

It was an alcoholic's best friend. The mother load of scotch.

Also in the bag was a little card with a handwritten note. *Have I got your attention yet?*, the note read.

I opened the cap and took a sniff. The aroma was glorious. One sip and I'd be back to square one.

I walked down to the water and poured out the entire quart. Then I rinsed the bottle in salt water and carried it back and tossed it into the trashcan.

I looked at the note again.

*Have I got your attention yet?*

I entered the trailer, made some coffee and sat at the table. "Yes," I said aloud. "You've got my attention."

My cell phone rang. It was Regan.

"Yes, hon," I said.

"Dad, Aunt Elizabeth and I are going to the mall," Regan said. "Do you want to meet us for lunch?"

"I have a few things I'm working on, sweetheart," I said. "I'll stop by the house later tonight."

"Okay, later then," Regan said.

I sat at the table for about an hour, working details over in my mind. Where did I slip up and alert Reed?

Who else but Reed could it be, and what was his next move?

Obviously, he knew he'd been hacked, and the three stooges he hired was a shot across the bow.

The bottle of scotch was his way of letting me know he'd done his homework.

As they say in the old murder mystery novels, the game was afoot.

Except that now the game was by Reed's rules, and I was no longer in control.

Exhaustion claimed my logic and I went to my bedroom and sprawled out on the bed still fully dressed.

* * *

Three hours later, I woke up and stumbled to the kitchen. The coffee in the pot was cold and stale, so I made some fresh and while it brewed, I went to the bathroom.

I brushed my teeth, washed my face, and took a good look in the mirror.

Where did I screw up? What was my mistake? How do I correct it?

I returned to the kitchen, filled a mug with fresh coffee and sat at the table. I glanced at my phone. Jane had called. I called her back.

"We picked up the third stooge about an hour ago," Jane said. "I'll be off at five and can be there by five-thirty."

"I have to go out," I said.

"Back when?"

"I don't know."

"Okay Bekker, what's going on?"

"Jane, just trust me," I said.

"To do what?"

"Just… trust me," I said.

I heard Jane sigh and exhale cigarette smoke at the same time. "Alright, but you call me later."

"I will," I said.

I hung up and then the world imploded.

# Chapter Forty-one

While I was sitting there at the table, sipping coffee, wishing I had a cigarette and trying to figure out how to reattach my head to my neck, the damndest thing happened.

The computer and monitor turned itself on.

I stared at the monitor.

I hadn't touched anything and yet it had turned on.

Then came the kick to the gut.

I was suddenly looking at the face of Yann Michael Reed on the monitor.

He smiled and said, "Why, Mr. Bekker, you look like somebody just pissed all over your mama's grave."

I stared at him.

"Got your attention yet?" Reed said.

"Yes," I said.

"Good."

Reed paused to light a thin, brown cigarette. "Nasty habit," he said. "I understand you've just recently quit."

"Yes," I said with the feeling in my stomach that Reed knew everything there was to know about me.

"By the way, did you enjoy the scotch?" he said. "I figured you being such a whiskey priest and all would appreciate a really fine scotch."

"I poured it out into the ocean," I said.

"Pity," Reed said. "After so many years of drinking, it must be really boring being sober all the time."

"It has its moments," I said.

I kept my questions to myself. Reed was enjoying himself far too much for me to ruin his mood. If I pushed, he might shut off.

"In case you're wondering, and I know you are, if you're going to hack a hacker, it's not wise to fall asleep and leave yourself logged in," Reed said. "It opens up a really large can of worms."

The monitor split in half. Reed was on the right, and a video of Wally sleeping at the table showed on the left.

"It didn't take me long to find out who sleeping beauty is," Reed said. "Wallace Sample, heir to Sample Ice Tea. What do you think would happen if this video went public?"

I remained silent.

"Don't like that video," Reed said. "How about this one?"

Wally vanished and was replaced with Jane, naked and writhing on my lap in the kitchen.

I closed my eyes.

"Upset your sensibilities?" Reed said.

I opened my eyes.

"What do you think would happen to the career of the county sheriff if this tape went viral?" Reed said.

"You made your point. Now turn it off," I said.

Reed filled the monitor again. "Now, let me tell you what I want," he said. "I want Captain Grimes to plead guilty in open court tomorrow and take the plea deal. If he doesn't, his wife and your daughter will never be heard from again."

The monitor screen split again and a dark image of Elizabeth and Regan appeared. They were bound and gagged.

"Ah, you got to love the mall," Reed said. "So many people and nobody ever sees a thing."

"Please don't hurt my daughter!" I shouted.

"Anymore than *you* already have?" Reed said. "I got to tell you, this is one fucked up kid you got. The screaming, not to mention she tried to beat her head against the wall. Thank goodness the captain's wife was there to comfort her."

"Please. Anything you say, just don't hurt her," I said.

"Ah, the submissive dog at last," Reed said. "Ever observe two male dogs meeting for the first time? They circle and sniff each other and then one submits to the other. One gets down in the submissive position and then just like that, it's over. One dog always quits. The alpha dog always wins."

Reed filled the screen again.

"What do you want me to do?" I said.

"First, get Captain Grimes to agree to the plea agreement and I'll release his wife," Reed said.

"And my daughter?" I said.

"She's my insurance policy," Reed said. "I will be leaving the country, permanently. I want your assurance my accounts won't be fucked with for seventy-two hours, and your daughter will be returned safe and sound. Agreed?"

"Yes."

"You have two hours," Reed said. "Call me at this number. It's a disposable cell phone, so it can't be traced."

I wrote the number down on a slip of paper.

"No cops, no FBI, just you," Reed said. "Or you'll never find the bodies. Go, little doggie, go."

The monitor went dark.

I jumped up, grabbed my keys and cell phone, and raced out the door.

In the car, I called Carly. "No questions," I said. "Get Kagan and meet me at my house right away. I'll explain everything there, but hurry. There isn't much time."

"Time for what?" Carly said just as I hung up.

* * *

"He's got my wife?" Walt said. "How the fuck does he have Elizabeth and Regan?

We were in the backyard with Carly, Kagan and Oz.

"Walt, there isn't time to explain," I said.

"The guy who framed me kidnapped Elizabeth and Regan?" Walt

said. "Is that what you're telling me? And I got to plead guilty to a crime I didn't commit to get them back? *Is that what you're telling me?*"

"Walt, calm down," Carly said.

Walt glared at me.

"I'm sorry," I said.

"You're sorry? You're fucking *sorry*?" Walt said.

"Walt, we don't have time for this," I said.

Walt lunged for me and threw a punch with his right fist. I sidestepped it and looked at Walt as he spun around.

"You son of a bitch," Walt said and swung a haymaker at me.

I ducked and stepped back.

"Fuck," Walt said and charged me like a bull.

He hit me low and pushed me backward.

"Walt, stop!" Carly shouted.

"He ain't gonna stop," Oz said.

Walt punched me in the stomach, screaming as he drove his fist into my gut.

"Walt, stop!" Carly screamed again.

"Bekker, put him down, man," Oz said. "He ain't gonna stop."

I took a step backward and launched a right uppercut to Walt's chin that snapped his head back, and then I followed through with a right to the jaw that ended it.

I caught Walt before he hit the ground, and gently set him onto a chair at the patio table.

Oz, always ready, handed Walt a glass of water.

Carly sat beside Walt. "Are you okay?"

Walt glared at me. "No thanks to this asshole," he said.

"Call him all the names you want later, but right now, you have to decide on saving your wife and Regan," Carly said.

"Of course I'll take the plea," Walt said. "What man wouldn't save his wife and a young girl?"

Carly looked at me. "Make the call."

I punched in the number Reed gave me and he answered on the third ring.

"He's agreed," I said.

"Of course he's agreed," Reed said. "Captain Grimes is a dedicated civil servant and a good family man. Put your phone on speaker."

I hit the speaker button.

"Captain Grimes, can you hear me?" Reed said.

"Yes," Walt said.

"Do you remember me now?" Reed said.

"I remember you," Walt said.

"I spent seven years in a Florida sweatbox for a victimless crime because of you," Reed said. "I lost my wife, my family, and my home, and now you're going to know what that feels like. Tomorrow morning you're going to plead guilty in open court. Agreed?"

"Yes," Walt said.

"I'll release your wife, but if you double-cross me, the girl dies, and no one will ever find me or her again," Reed said. "Understand?"

"Yes," Walt said.

"Bekker, take the phone off speaker," Reed said.

I hit the speaker button again and put the phone to my ear.

"After dark, drive to the parking lot of the Wind Chimes Motel off exit nine on the highway," Reed said. "It's abandoned, so it will be nice and quiet. The wife is in the back of a van. It will be unlocked. And a camera will see everything, so if you're thinking of bringing anybody with you, just think of your little girl."

"I'll be alone," I said.

"And I'll be watching," Reed said. "I'll call you after he pleads."

The phone went dead and I stuck it in my pocket.

I looked at Walt. "Don't worry, Walt, I'll get Elizabeth back," I said. "After dark, I'll be back with her."

* * *

"On top of everything else, he has a video of us?" Jane said. "You asshole. You absolute fucking asshole."

"Call me names later," I said. "Are you going to back me or not?"

"Of course, I'm going to back you, you moron," Jane said.

"What do you have in your cruiser?" I said.

"Pistol grip 12-gauge," Jane said.

I stood from the kitchen table in the trailer and went to my bedroom, unlocked the Benelli M4 shotgun from the wall and brought it and a box of shells back to the table.

"Use this," I said.

Jane picked up the shotgun. "Where did you get this thing?"

"A grateful client who was a collector," I said.

"Give me a minute to change," Jane said.

# Chapter Forty-two

Wearing black jeans, a black T-shirt, and black sneakers, Jane sat beside me in my car and smoked a cigarette.

"So how bad is this video?" she said.

"Bad."

"When I…?"

"Yup."

"And when you…?"

"Yup."

Jane blew a smoke ring out her open window. "We'll talk about it later," she said.

"If it's any consolation, you look really great on film," I said.

Jane shook her head. "Asshole," she said and blew another smoke ring.

* * *

Off exit nine, I followed the road to the dark, deserted motel. A block before the parking lot, Jane put on a black ski mask and climbed over the seat to the rear.

I didn't need to tell her to keep her head low, Jane was an experienced professional.

I entered the parking lot and stopped about a hundred feet behind the van.

"If the van explodes, find Reed wherever he is and kill him for me," I said.

Tucked down below the seat, Jane said, "Love to."

I opened my car door, stepped out and looked at the motel. It had been abandoned for some time and was close to being condemned.

I walked to the van and cautiously opened the rear door.

Elizabeth, bound and gagged with duct tape, was asleep on the floor of the van. I gently shook her shoulder. She woke up and started flailing and screaming inside the duct tape.

"Liz, it's Jack," I said. "It's me Bekker."

With wide eyes filled with fear, Elizabeth looked at me. Recognition set in and she calmed down. I used my pocketknife to cut the duct tape from her legs and arms, and then slowly removed the piece from her mouth.

"He's got Regan," she said.

"I know. It will be alright. Can you walk?" I said.

"I think so."

She tried, but her legs were weak, so I carried Elizabeth to the car and placed her in the back seat.

"Sheriff Morgan?" Elizabeth said and burst into tears.

"Jack, go, she's coming apart," Jane said.

I raced back to the highway.

Jane sat up and held Elizabeth around the shoulders.

"We were… we were going to the car and he came out of nowhere," Elizabeth said. "He grabbed me from behind and put a rag over my face. The next thing I knew I woke up in the back of that van."

"Was Regan with you?" I said.

"Yes, but he moved her. She fought like hell. She bit and scratched him and he slapped her," Elizabeth said.

"He slapped Regan?" I said.

"Yes, but she isn't hurt," Elizabeth said. "God, I feel sick."

I pulled over, and Elizabeth rushed out and vomited on the side of the road. Jane got out, and when Elizabeth quieted down, they returned to the car.

"Jack, give me that bottle of water you got there," Jane said.

I removed the water bottle from the cup holder and passed it to Jane.

"Here, take this," Jane said.

I glanced in the rearview mirror and watched as Jane gave something to Elizabeth and she took it with a sip of water.

About a mile from home, Elizabeth slumped over onto Jane's lap.

"What did you give her?" I said.

"Valium," Jane said.

"Why do you have Valium?" I said.

"You try being your girlfriend," Jane said.

By the time I reached my driveway, Elizabeth was out for the count. I carried her into the house and Carly opened the door.

"She's hurt," Walt said as he rushed to us.

"I gave her a Valium," Jane said. "She's not hurt."

"Jack, the bedroom," Carly said.

* * *

We gathered at the picnic table with mugs of coffee.

"Jack, after Walt takes the plea and you get Regan back, I'm going straight to the FBI," Carly said.

"I agree," Kagan said. "They started this mess with their false information, they can end it."

"If I have one more night of freedom, I'm spending it with my wife," Walt said, stood up and entered the house.

"I guess we should meet at the courthouse around nine-thirty," Carly said.

"Try and get some sleep," Kagan said. "Regan will be alright and you'll have her back tomorrow."

I looked at Kagan.

"You know, I have some Italian friends who owe me some favors," Kagan said.

"We'll talk about that some other time, Frank," Carly said.

After Carly and Kagan left, Oz said, "I'm going to turn in. Bekker, you'll get her back tomorrow. Don't worry."

"Sure," I said.

Oz went inside, leaving just Jane at the table with me. "I have to make transport arrangements for Walt in the morning," she said.

"No," I said. "You and I can bring him in my car. You're the sheriff, you have the authority. Why make it a media circus?"

Jane nodded. "Alright, but you drive and I sit in back with Walt," she said.

It was my turn to nod. "If Regan is hurt in any way, I will hunt him down and kill him," I said.

"And I will help you, but right now let's try to get some rest," Jane said.

"All that's left is the daybed in the basement," I said.

Jane stood up and took my hand.

"That will do," she said.

* * *

Reed may be an insane genius, but he wasn't entirely wrong when he said much of Regan's condition was my fault.

When Regan was just five-years-old, Walt and I were part of a large task force investigating organized crime.

I got too close and a killer was sent to my house to dispatch a warning. Except I wasn't home and he took it out on my wife, Carol. He killed her, and Regan, hiding in a closet, had to witness it.

It left her traumatized and she spent the next twelve years living in a hospital for traumatized children.

I fell into a bottle of scotch, retired from the job, and neglected Regan for a decade.

It was safe to say that Regan's condition—and my lot in life—was mostly my fault.

In the dark, Jane said, "Jack, stop thinking so much and try to sleep."

"If she's hurt…" I said.

"She won't be," Jane said. "You have to believe that. Now get some sleep or you'll be useless come tomorrow."

I closed my eyes with the feeling I'd been useless most of my adult life.

# Chapter Forty-three

Oz and Elizabeth rode with Carly and Kagan in the limo. Wearing a clean suit, Walt stood before Jane.

"I'm ready," he said.

"Walt, I don't know what to say," I said.

"For better or worse, right?" Walt said. "Just make sure you get her back safe."

"I won't put the cuffs on until we reach the courthouse," Jane said.

"I appreciate that, Jane," Walt said.

* * *

Walt, Carly, Kagan and Harry stood at their table and looked at Judge Foss, who was behind the bench.

Napier stood alone at the prosecutor's table.

Jane stood off to the side with two court officers.

"I've closed the courtroom to avoid a media circus," Foss said. "However, I must caution you about grandstanding to the media afterward on the courtroom steps, *both* the People and the defense. Am I clear on this?"

"Yes, your honor," Carly said.

"Yes, your honor," Napier said.

"Mr. Napier, are you satisfied with the defense's plea?" Foss said.

"The People are satisfied, your honor," Napier said.

"Captain Grimes, do you have anything to say before I close the book on this?" Foss said.

"May I have five minutes to say goodbye to my wife?" Walt said.

"I'll allow it," Foss said.

"Thank you, your honor," Walt said.

"Captain Grimes, you are to serve a minimum of seven years and no more than ten years at a prison to be determined within thirty days," Foss said. "Court is adjourned."

* * *

While Elizabeth was in a Valium-induced sleep, Carly, Kagan, Oz and Jane sat at the patio table in my backyard.

Finally, my cell phone rang. I motioned for everyone to be quiet and answered the call on speaker.

"At least you're a man of your word," Reed said.

"My daughter?" I said.

"Unharmed and waiting," Reed said. "Remember our agreement?"

"Seventy-two hours, yes," I said.

"I'm about to board a plane," Reed said. "What airport and under what name, you'll never know. I'll call you after dark with instructions where to find your daughter."

The phone went dead in my hand.

"Jesus Christ," Kagan said.

"What time is sunset tonight?"

"Hold on," Oz said and went inside and returned with a newspaper.

"7:47," Oz said.

"He's not flying to the Cayman Islands," I said. "He'll call when he lands. Where is he going that he'll call in eight hours?"

"It could be anywhere, Jack," Carly said.

"I have something to do," I said.

* * *

I spread out all of Wally's documents on the table outside the trailer. Jane looked over my shoulder.

"Wally found all this?" she said.

"Wally is a genius in his own right," I said.

I shifted through the papers.

"Zurich," I said. "He's going to Zurich to close out his account. Then Switzerland and the big one in Prague."

"What about the accounts in the Caymans and the Bank of London?" Jane said.

"He'll keep those in reserve," I said. "Between Zurich, Switzerland and Prague he has eight million dollars. He'll set up a new account with that and keep the other accounts in reserve for an emergency."

"What are you planning, Jack?" Jane said. "You're not going to fly all over Europe looking for him, are you?"

"No."

I took a chair and Jane took the one next to me.

"After I get Regan back, have a team of your deputies raid the girlfriend's house, and the mother's, too," I said. "I doubt he left anything behind, but you never know."

"I'm going to the office to make arrangements," Jane said. "I'll meet you back here at seven-thirty."

After Jane left, I changed and went for an hour-long run along the water. Then worked the heavy bag and speed bag until I could hardly lift my arms.

I took a breather to drink some water, and then did elevated push-ups until my arms and chest gave out.

I returned to the heavy bag and beat on it until I had nothing left, and I collapsed to my knees in frustration.

Once I regained my breath, I stood and removed the bag gloves. Knuckles on both hands were bleeding.

After a shower and a change of clothes, I felt no better and still had three hours to sunset.

If I was bound, gagged, and dying from a thousand small cuts, the time couldn't have passed any slower.

An entire pot of coffee consumed the rest of the afternoon, and around seven-fifteen, I spotted Jane's cruiser on the sand.

She parked beside my car, got out, walked toward me and took a chair.

"As soon as we have Regan, two cruisers will respond to the girlfriend's house and two more to the mother's," she said.

"And you?"

"I'll be with you," Jane said.

I watched the sun touch down on the horizon, and the ocean glowed burnt orange for about ten minutes.

The sky darkened and the ocean went black.

Neither Jane nor I spoke until my cell phone rang. I hit the speaker button and Reed said, "At least Grimes has the balls to go down like a man."

"My daughter?" I said.

"You might want to write this down," Reed said.

"I'll remember."

"The Lock and Go Storage Facility, unit number thirty-seven. Bring a bolt cutter," Reed said. "Keypad is 67681. Goodbye, Mr. Bekker."

The phone went dead and I hung up.

"Do you have a bolt cutter?" I said to Jane.

"Who doesn't?" Jane said.

"You have a GPS?"

"Who doesn't?" Jane said.

"We'll take the cruiser," I said.

"I'll drive," Jane said.

# Chapter Forty-four

The Lock and Go Storage Facility was about an hour north and located at the end of a large business park.

There were one hundred garage-sized units. The entire facility was surrounded by a chain link fence with a motor-operated gate.

Jane pulled up beside the keypad. "What was that number?"

"67681."

She punched in the number and the gate slid open.

Jane drove us to unit thirty-seven. The facility was well lit with surveillance cameras in various locations.

Jane gave me the bolt cutter as we walked to the roll down door. It was secured at the midpoint by a heavy padlock on each side.

I sliced through the two locks and rolled up the door, not knowing what to expect.

Relief washed over me when Regan looked at me from the comfortable chair she was seated on and set the Harry Potter book she was reading on the table beside the chair.

There was a small refrigerator in the corner, and an overhead fan and cot with a pillow against the wall.

Regan smiled, jumped from the chair, ran to me, then leapt into my arms and wrapped her legs around my waist like she used to do as a child.

I was expecting her to be an emotional mess in need of the trauma center, and thank God, I was wrong.

"I knew you'd come," Regan said as I set her down. "Did you get Aunt Elizabeth?"

Choking back tears, I said, "She's fine. She's with Oz."

"I scratched him. Look. His skin is under my nails," Regan said. "And this."

Regan stuck her hand in a jeans pocket and showed me a dozen or so hairs.

"I yanked his hair from the roots," Regan said. "That's DNA, right?"

"Right," I said.

"Like father, like daughter," Jane said.

"Hey, Jane," Regan said.

"Hey, Regan," Jane said.

"Let's get you home," I said.

"Wait," Regan said. She grabbed her book and then went to the small refrigerator and retrieved a six pack of root beer.

I sat in back with Regan. The three of us drank root beer on the drive home.

"You're not hurt?" I said to Regan.

"No," Regan said. "When I woke up, I acted crazy to try to scare him. He slapped me, but he didn't hurt me."

"He slapped you?" I said.

"Uh-oh," Jane said as she sipped root beer.

"I pulled his hair and scratched him," Regan said. "I think he just wanted to make me stop. Aunt Elizabeth fought him like a tiger when she woke up. He had to tie her up and drug her to make her stop."

"Any idea where he took you?" Jane said.

"No, the both of us were asleep," Regan said.

"It doesn't matter," I said.

When we reached home and Regan hugged Oz, he broke down in tears.

"I'm alright, Oz," she said. "Hungry, though. I'm gonna take a shower and fix something to eat."

"Let's order out," I said. "Anything you want."

"Pizza," Regan said. "Lots and lots of pizza."

While Regan took a shower and Oz ordered Pizza, Jane and I sat at the patio table in the backyard and I called Carly.

"Thank God she's safe," Carly said. "That sick son of a bitch needs to be put down, Jack."

"Any word from Foss on prison selection for Walt?" I said.

"Too soon, Jack."

"I'm losing track of time," I said.

"I'll call Foss tomorrow and get back to you," Carly said.

"Thanks," I said.

After I hung up, Jane lit a cigarette and said, "So, what are you gonna do?"

I heard the front doorbell ring and the pug bark.

"Eat some pizza," I said.

* * *

Jane's deputies picked up Reed's mother, who went kicking and screaming. A search of her house produced nothing.

I went with Jane and a team of her deputies to Reed's girlfriend's house. She was gone and so were her clothes, along with the computer in the basement. Riker had either gone with Reed to Europe, or he had killed her and cleaned house.

* * *

I opted to spend the night at the trailer with Jane.

"Is that thing on?" she said as she looked at the computer.

"I unplugged it," I said.

"I'm not sure I forgive you yet for the video thing," Jane said.

"I haven't forgiven myself yet for this entire mess," I said. "Walt's in jail awaiting prison, his wife and my daughter were the ransom to get Walt to confess to a crime he didn't commit, and Reed is in Europe laughing all the way to the bank."

"Can't he appeal now that his wife and Regan are safe?" Jane said. "I'll testify to the kidnapping. Carly and Kagan can talk to the judge. There is enough evidence to have Walt's confession overturned in court."

"Maybe," I said. "And maybe Walt does seven years."

Jane looked at the computer. "Are you sure it's off?"

"It's not plugged in," I said.

Jane took my hand. "Good, I need to relieve some stress," she said, and walked us to my bedroom.

* * *

Carly, Kagan and I met with Walt at the county jail where he was being held in isolation.

"We're meeting with Judge Foss tomorrow morning to explain your guilty plea and request your release," Carly said. "We have enough evidence for the FBI to pursue Reed for everything. Extortion, fraud, kidnapping, all of it."

"And if he can't be found?" Walt said.

"After reviewing all the evidence, what else can Foss do but let you out?" Carly said.

Walt looked at me. "Jack?"

"The files Wally put together prove Reed's guilt without a doubt," I said.

"Sit tight," Carly said. "Let the system work."

"It's done a great job so far," Walt said.

* * *

"Oz, do you still have that shotgun?" I said.

"It's under my bed," Oz said. "Why?"

"Keep it handy. Keep it loaded," I said. "I'll be gone for a few days."

"I suppose it won't do me no good to ask where?" Oz said.

"I'll call you and let you know," I said. "In the meantime, take care of Regan and Elizabeth."

"You gotta ask?" Oz said.

"No," I said. "I don't gotta ask."

We were at the patio table in the backyard. The kitchen door slid open and Regan came out, followed by Molly and the pug.

"Honey, I need those hairs you took from Reed," I said.

"I put them in a baggie," Regan said.

"Can you get them for me?" I asked.

"Sure. Why, what are you going to do?" Regan said.

"See if an old friend is still an old friend," I said.

# Chapter Forty-five

Paul Lawrence lived in Alexandria, Virginia, about forty minutes south of D.C.

I flew into Regan International, rented a car, and drove to Alexandria.

Paul lived in a nice house on a cul-de-sac in a quiet neighborhood.

I arrived at his house around seven-thirty at night. A dark sedan was parked in the driveway. I parked behind it, got out with the thick file under my arm, walked to the door, and rang the bell.

Paul was genuinely shocked to see me when he answered the door.

"What the hell are you doing here?" he said.

"Good to see you, too," I said.

"Don't give me that," Paul said. "I told you no more favors, old friends or not."

"I'm not here for a favor," I said.

"Then what?"

"Can I come in?"

* * *

Paul had a nice lawn in the backyard. We sat at the patio table and he read my files by the light from an outside floodlight. We each had a mug of coffee.

When he was done, Paul closed the file. He sipped from his mug and looked at me. "It certainly is enough to open an investigation," he said.

"Investigation my ass," I said. "Walt is sitting in county lockup while we sit here drinking your gourmet coffee."

"What do you suggest?" Paul said.

"We grab an FBI plane to Europe and bring his ass back for trial," I said.

"We?" Paul said.

"It's a hell of an arrest for the FBI *and* for you," I said. "You get a really bad guy and Walt goes free. It's a win-win for everybody."

Paul looked at me and sighed.

"Oh, and this," I said. I pulled the baggie with Reed's hair in it from my jacket pocket. "Regan pulled it from him when he kidnapped her. The roots are intact for DNA testing."

Paul looked at me.

"What more do you want, an engraved invitation from the Queen of England?" I said.

"I'll need the tech boys to…" Paul said.

"We don't need the tech boys," I said. "All we need is an FBI jet."

Paul sighed. "Let me call the boss," he said.

* * *

Halfway across the Atlantic, I called Wally at his home in White Plains.

"Hi Mr. Bekker, I wasn't expecting you to call," Wally said. "I was just watching a show about lions on the…"

"Wally, listen carefully," I said. "I need your help."

"I'll get dressed," Wally said.

"No, not that kind of…" I said.

"I think better when I'm dressed," Wally said. "Hold on."

I looked at Paul. "He's getting dressed," I said.

"By all means," Paul said.

I switched the phone to speaker while we waited.

"Okay, I'm back," Wally said. "I'm missing a sock, though."

"Never mind the… Wally, listen carefully," I said.

"The lions just ate a gazelle," Wally said.

"Wally, focus," I said.

"Okay, okay, what do you need?" Wally said.

"Can you…" I said.

"I found the sock," Wally said.

"For God's sake, Wally. Focus," I said.

"Okay, okay, I'm focused. What do you need me to do?" Wally said.

"Can you tell me which accounts Reed had that have been closed?" I said.

"Not without all the codes I gave you. Did you lose them?"

"No, Wally, I didn't lose them," I said. "Are you near a computer?"

"I have one in my home office," Wally said.

"Are you in your home office?" I said.

"What, no. Oh, right, hold on," Wally said.

I looked at Paul. His face showed disbelief. I shrugged.

"Okay, okay, I'm at my desk," Wally said.

"I want you to check the accounts in Zurich, Germany and Prague," I said.

"Okay, give me the account numbers and call me back in thirty minutes," Wally said.

"Thirty minutes," I said.

I hung up and Paul said, "In thirty minutes, we'll be halfway to France."

"What do you have to eat on this thing?" I said. "Neither of us has had breakfast."

The galley was loaded with food. Paul nuked egg sandwiches and made fresh coffee. We also each had a large Danish and orange juice.

At the thirty-minute mark, I called Wally.

"Mr. Bekker, I checked the accounts," Wally said.

I waited, counted to ten and then said, "And the results are?"

"What? Oh, yeah, the results," Wally said. "Zurich and Switzerland have been closed, but the account in Prague is still active."

"Thank you, Wally," I said. "Thank you very much."

"The lions got another one," Wally said.

"They always do," I said. "Goodnight, Wally."

I hung up and looked at Paul.

"Prague it is," Paul said.

# Chapter Forty-six

Paul handed me a container of thick Czech coffee. We were inside a Prague undercover van that was parked across the street from the National Bank of Prague.

Two members of the Prague Police Department were in the van with us. They were high-ranking detectives and both spoke English.

Both were smoking Turkish unfiltered cigarettes.

"The bank opens in fifteen minutes," one of the detectives said.

Surveillance cameras fed into a bank of monitors inside the van, and we watched them for signs of Reed.

"It's been two days, how do you know he'll show at all?" the other detective said.

"Because he wants his money," I said. "He wants to close his account and go live the good life, and in order to close the account, he needs to be here in person to do it."

"Jack," Paul said.

We looked at the monitor. Wearing an expensive suit, Reed walked up the steps to the bank and waited for the doors to open.

One of the detectives picked up a radio.

"No," I said. "On the way out."

Reed was in the bank for over an hour.

I drank some of the Czech coffee. It went down like turpentine. The Prague detectives chain-smoked their Turkish cigarettes. We watched the monitor. I counted the number of steps from the sidewalk to the bank. There were thirty-five.

Then Reed finally appeared at the top of the steps.

I slid open the side door of the van and hopped out.

Paul and the two detectives followed.

We stood off to the side on the crowded sidewalk and watched as Reed started down the thirty-five steps.

When he reached the tenth step from the bottom I broke away.

Behind me I heard Paul say, "No, it's his show."

On the fifth step to the bottom, I cut in front of Reed.

For a moment, he was startled. Then recognition set in and his eyes went as wide as tea cups.

I grabbed Reed by the front of his suit jacket and pulled him close.

"Remember the story you told me about the two dogs?" I said. "Well, I'm not your average dog and I *never* submit."

I flung Reed down the steps and he landed at Paul's feet.

Paul looked up at me.

"Now let's go get Walt out of jail," I said.

# About the Author

Al Lamanda is a native of New York City. His mystery novels include *Dunston Falls*, *Walking Homeless*, *Running Homeless*, *Sunset*, *Sunrise*, *First Light*, *This Side of Midnight*, *With Six You Get Wally* and *Who Killed Joe Italiano?*. He has been nominated for the Edgar Award and the Nero Award for his mysteries, and was selected as the 2017 Nero Award winner for his John Bekker crime novel, *With Six You Get Wally*.